Mickey R. Thompson

CONFIDENTIAL

COBRA FILES

Case no. 20-8-5/19-5-3-18-5-20/

1-7-5-14-20-19

Operation: Vanishing Agents

Status: **TOP SECRET**

3

D0995331

For Alasdair

OXFORD
UNIVERSITY PRESS

Great Clarendon Street, Oxford OX2 6DP

Oxford University Press is a department of the University of Oxford. It furthers the University's objective of excellence in research, scholarship, and education by publishing worldwide.

Oxford is a registered trade mark of Oxford University Press in the UK and in certain other countries

Database right Oxford University Press (maker)

First published 2021

British Library Cataloguing in Publication Data

Data available

ISBN: 978-0-19-277365-4

1 3 5 7 9 10 8 6 4 2

Printed in India by Manipal Technologies Limited

Paper used in the production of this book is a natural, recyclable product made from wood grown in sustainable forests. The manufacturing process conforms to the environmental regulations of the country of origin.

MICKEY

·:· AND THE ·:·

MISSING SPY

ANNE MILLER

Illustrated by
BECKA MOOR

OXFORD
UNIVERSITY PRESS

Briefing sheet

COBRA is a secret group of animal spies tasked with protecting the world's animals from dangers that humans can't even imagine. Run by a cobra named Coby, the group's High Committee includes a human liaison officer—a human girl called Mickey. She has worked hard to earn the respect of COBRA after they were betrayed by her predecessor, a man named Harry.

Mickey's hero is a retired human agent called Hildegarde L. McTavish. Recently, Harry tried to break into an Impossible Vault designed by Hildegarde and though Mickey and the animal spies foiled his plans, Harry managed to escape the vault with a mysterious folder.

Harry's whereabouts are currently unknown . . .

MICKEY

Human

COBRA's Human
Liaison Officer

Likes: Code-cracking, The life and work of Secret Agent and Codebreaker Extraordinaire Hildegarde L. McTavish, Gymnastics

Dislikes: Beetroot, Harry—COBRA's former human liaison officer

COBY

Snake

Head of COBRA

Likes: Order, Rules, Success

Dislikes: Disobedience, Cold weather, Harry

CLARKE

Cat

Head of
Domestic
Animals (Pets)

Likes: Feeling superior, Mealtimes

Dislikes: Animals who walk too
slowly, Animals who aren't cats, Harry

ASTRID

Spider Monkey

Head of
International
Animals

Likes: Grapes, Going on missions
with Mickey, Swinging from things

Dislikes: Arguments, Harry

TILDA

Sloth

Temporary
Member

(a post that swaps
between different animals)

<u>Likes:</u> Sleeping, Eating, Being still

<u>Dislikes:</u> Sprinting, Harry

RUPERT

Rat

Head of
Wild Animals

<u>Likes:</u> Rodents, Art, Literature

<u>Dislikes:</u> Those without a sporting
nature, Reaching things on the top
shelf, Harry

BERTIE

Giraffe

Security Guard

<u>Likes:</u> Reaching things on the
top shelf, Being part of the gang,
Bow ties

<u>Dislikes:</u> Harry

Chapter

1

Mickey was crouched on the floor,
in the middle of a long dark corridor
that was studded with bright laser
beams. She'd slipped easily under the
first two, carefully holding onto her
ponytail to make sure it didn't swing
out, hit the beam, and trip the alarm.

The next laser was giving her cause for concern because it kept switching positions. One minute it was a diagonal line facing in one direction then it flipped and ran the other way. Mickey breathed in deeply and let her breath out slowly. She knew she'd have to time this very carefully if she wanted to make it safely through to the other side. She carefully counted the seconds to work out how long she would have. '. . . seven, eight, nine, and *switch*,' she muttered, watching as the beam changed position again. Once it was holding the new shape, Mickey crawled forwards, keeping as close to the wall as she possibly could, her elbows tucked in and her head low. She was rewarded with the overwhelming feeling of both elation and relief as she reached the other side. A split second later the laser crackled and switched position again.

'Nice work,' came a voice from just above her head. It was Astrid, the spider monkey who was the Head of International Animals for **COBRA**, the secret group of animal spies that Mickey also belonged to. Astrid was hanging off a light fitting with her long limbs and swinging herself backwards and forwards to build up momentum to jump across to the next light and skip the laser business altogether.

'It's not that difficult really,' drawled Clarke the cat's voice from much further down the corridor. 'I've made it through all the lasers, and to be quite honest, I'm growing tired of waiting for you all to catch up!'

'You haven't been there that long,' called Rupert the rat, who was also near the end of the course. 'And as you're a cat it's easier for you. Mickey and Bertie are much larger so are at a height disadvantage.'

Mickey looked behind her to see Bertie the giraffe still near the beginning of the course and looking nervous.

11

'Come on Bertie, you can do it,' she called encouragingly. 'Just watch out for your tail! And Tilda, how are you doing?'

'I'm going as fast as I can,' came the sloth's voice. She was even further behind, still at the entrance door they'd all walked through some time ago.

'We're going to be trapped here for days,' Mickey heard Clarke mutter. 'And it's way past my meal time. I think I can feel starvation kicking in.'

'Clarke,' said Mickey, 'your stomach is *not* our number one priority right now. We all need to get through as a team, so perhaps your time would be better spent helping Bertie and Tilda.'

'I . . . I d-don't think I can do it,' called Bertie, his voice wobbling. 'I'm just too tall and my neck keeps getting in the way.'

'You can do it Bertie,' called Astrid.

'I quite concur,' added Rupert. 'Just plan your move carefully and then commit.'

'Okay,' came the giraffe's reply. 'I'll just

ah . . .

12

ah…

    argh, oh no, my tail.'

Mickey watched in horror as Bertie's tail swung out and flicked the laser beam. She winced and clamped her hands over her ears to protect them from the alarm, but the room stayed silent.

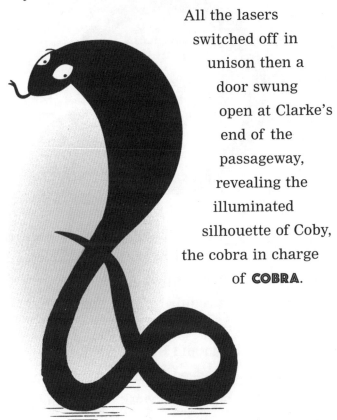

All the lasers switched off in unison then a door swung open at Clarke's end of the passageway, revealing the illuminated silhouette of Coby, the cobra in charge of **COBRA**.

Coby flicked a switch on the wall with her tail and then, with a click, the overhead fluorescent lighting flickered to life. Coby reached out her tail for the stopwatch hanging around the hooded part of her neck.

'Four minutes, 23 and a half seconds,' said Coby. 'Clarke and Rupert you completed the course, excellent work. Astrid, you were nearly there but require a little more speed next time, please. Mickey, not bad for a human. And Tilda and Bertie, we need to see more agility and speed from the pair of you. Bertie, you've done good work controlling your neck but you must now concentrate on your tail. Remember, we are an elite group of spies, agility under pressure is a must, hence this training exercise. In a practice run, a mistake like that just means the timer stops, but in real life, it could be a life or death situation.'

'I'll keep practising Coby,' promised the giraffe faithfully, and Mickey smiled to herself. If you'd told her a year ago that she'd be on a training exercise with a group of animal spies she wouldn't have believed it, but that's what is so wonderful about the unexpected. You don't see it coming.

Chapter

2

'Follow me,' hissed Coby, leading them through into their meeting room. Their usual table had been pushed to one side of the room to maximize floor space and there was an enormous whiteboard attached to the far wall. Written on the board was a string of symbols which Mickey quickly recognized as a code.

'Snacks will be served when the code is cracked,' announced Coby, as she slithered to the back of the room. 'No solution, no food. Your time begins . . . now!'

All the animals immediately turned to look hopefully at Mickey. The smaller and faster animals might have had the advantage in agility, but cracking codes was Mickey's special skill.

'Can you do it?' asked Astrid. She slipped a pen into Mickey's hand as all the other animals watched eagerly.

Mickey approached the puzzle in her favourite way. She stood back and looked at it carefully, taking in all the details. She knew there was a way to crack it—she just needed to land on the key. She scanned the image carefully from left to right and up and down in case there were any additional clues.

'Oh,' she said as something lit up in her brain. 'I know what this is, it's a pigpen puzzle! You just need the right code to decipher it. I think I remember the key.'

'Excellent work my dear,' cried Rupert clapping his paws.

Mickey smiled, and using the pen Astrid had slipped her, she quickly approached the whiteboard and scrawled out the key to the puzzle.

She had read about pigpen codes and had tried them out before. To create the key you had to fill the letters of the alphabet into four different grids—two with dots and two without. Once you had this, it was just a matter of comparing the shapes and working out which letters were represented in the code.

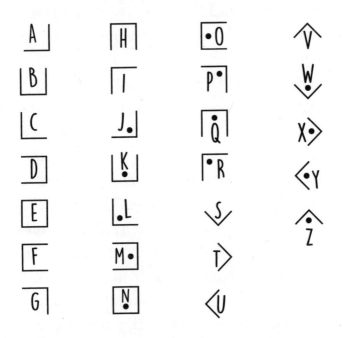

'So, the first letter is a box with a dot in,' said Mickey, looking between the code and the key. 'So that's an "N".'

Then she worked her way through the message translating the string of jumbled symbols into words. Mickey stood back and read her answer:

⬚ꓩꓶꛯ ꛎꏂꓞꛃ ꓱꓩꓶꛃꛯ⟨
'NICE WORK MICKEY,' she said.

'Indeed,' said Coby, 'that was certainly speedy work. And I had a fairly strong idea of who would solve the puzzle the fastest, no offence, Tilda.'

The sloth nodded slowly and good-naturedly from her spot near the back of the room. Mickey always thought one of the best things about **COBRA** was how each animal was celebrated for their own traits and talents. Tilda might not excel at speed, but she was the best of the team at staying still and quiet while on a stakeout. All the High Committee were equally committed to their **COBRA** work and to standing up for the world's animals, whatever trouble they may find themselves in.

'And now,' said Coby, 'it's time for some refreshments.'

'Finally', said Clarke.

Chapter

3

Bertie was handing out the food as the other **COBRA** members were sitting at their meeting table, now moved back into the centre of the room.

Mickey opened the lid on her dish and jumped straight out of her seat in shock as the smell hit her nose.

'Oh!' she yelped, slamming the lid back down. Her box was full of what looked like peelings and scrapings from a kitchen bin that had been left to ferment.

'Oh, you've got mine,' said Rupert cheerily. 'I must have yours.' He slid the dish that was in front of him down to Mickey and signalled to her to do the same. 'Ah, bins! What a treat.'

'Oh,' Mickey shuddered, reaching gratefully for the new container. Cautiously she opened it and was immediately hit with the overwhelming scent of tuna. 'Clarke, have I got yours?' she called.

'Fish!!!' said the cat, his usually distinguished demeanour slipping as he caught sight of his favourite food. 'And perhaps you know what this is?' he asked as he rolled a large papaya between his paws.

'My favourite!' said Astrid, scampering over to grab it.

Mickey finally traced her own plate of cheese, crackers and an apple. It was in front of Bertie who was staring at it curiously.

Mickey spotted his platter of leaves sitting out in the corridor where he'd left it and went to collect it for him.

'Bertie, are you alright?' she asked as she approached him. The giraffe let out a long sigh and looked down at his feet, which were a considerable distance away from his head.

'I don't mind running the office security, but I so badly want to be an agent and work in the field with the rest of you. Sometimes I worry I'll never get there and the laser test today proved it. Perhaps I should just stick to desk duties.'

'Not at all,' said Mickey, setting down the plate of leaves in front of him. 'You're an excellent security guard, and I bet you'll make an even better agent once you get the hang of it. When I joined they said I'd never last and now we've solved two missions together—Operation Shiny Dog and Operation Mischievous Moles. You'll do it too, I just know it!'

'Do you really think so?' said Bertie.

'Yes,' said Mickey, smiling. 'Your dreams

will come true just like mine have. Did
you know that I even got a letter from my
favourite codemaker of all time—**Hildegarde
L. McTavish?!'**

'Oh yes, I remember hearing that,' said
Bertie. 'And she said she would be in touch
again. Have you heard anything?'

'Not yet,' said Mickey, reaching for the
letter which she had been carrying around
in her pocket ever since it had arrived. It
was quite crumpled now and had been read
many, many times, but
she still couldn't
quite believe her
hero knew her
name and
had taken the
time to write
to her.

Dear Mickey,

I received word that The Impossible Vault was recently breached and that you were the one to do it. Don't worry, you aren't in any trouble, I've heard all about how you were working to save your pet rat. He is lucky to have you.

I am so pleased you have a passion for codebreaking. Perhaps you might like to meet up when I am back in the country? My travels will take me away for a few months but meeting a fellow codebreaker would bring me a great deal of joy.

Though perhaps stay away from bank break-ins in future. (Even for the best of reasons.)

Very best wishes,

Hildegarde L. McTavish

PS—and always remember that when life gives you lemons you must make lemonade!

Hildegarde L. McTavish had been a top-level human spy in her day. She was one of the greatest codebreakers and codemakers of her generation, and she was Mickey's hero. She had read Hildegarde's book *Cracking the Codes* so many times she knew the contents off by heart.

When Mickey had finished reading the letter for the first time, she had recognized the smell of lemons immediately, and taking the hint from the PS about lemonade, she had wondered if the message was hiding more words written in invisible ink, as she knew that Hildegarde had her own recipe based around lemon juice. Mickey had applied heat to the page (which she'd read was often the key to unveiling invisible ink) and revealed two extra words which were now incredibly faint but still ran along the top of the letter. They said 'HELP ME'.

At first Mickey had worried Hildegarde was in trouble and then she'd wondered if it was some sort of request for assistance with a case—after all, she had been hired by **COBRA** after she'd spotted a mysterious code on a bus—Mickey knew more than most people that things which sounded impossible very often weren't. You just had to look at them from a different angle.

'I hope she's in touch soon,' said Bertie, who seemed cheered and was now chomping through his leaves.

Mickey didn't know how the news of her codebreaking skills had reached Hildegarde, but she suspected the spy wasn't as retired as people thought she was. Mickey was desperate to meet Hildegarde in real life. She loved being part of the animal spy world, but the idea of being able to discuss cases and tips with someone from the human spy world was an indescribably wonderful thought.

'She hasn't been in contact yet,' said Mickey, 'but hopefully it won't be much longer.' Mickey knew that Hildegarde considered patience to be a virtue so she would just have to sit tight.

'It's not how long you wait but how you conduct yourself while you are waiting which shows your true skill.'

Cracking the Codes by Hildegarde L. McTavish

Mickey had been putting Hildegarde's advice into practice for years. Waiting with her coat and shoes on for her parents to be ready to head out for their weekly food shop, or when the programme she wanted to watch wasn't due out for another 35 minutes, or when the chocolate cookies in the oven needed ten minutes to cool even though she was desperate to eat them straight away. She had learned this lesson the hard way when she ate them too early, burned her tongue, and wound up feeling much more uncomfortable than the short wait would have felt had she had more patience. However, waiting for Hildegarde to get back in touch felt like the longest wait. In. The. *Universe*.

'Hopefully, it won't be too much longer,' she repeated, to reassure herself as much as the animals. She couldn't rule out the option that this was another test, and if it was a test of her own patience, she was determined to pass, no matter how uncomfortable and

sloooooooow

it felt in the meantime.

Chapter

4

After the training session finished, Mickey walked home, thinking of Hildegarde. As she neared her family's flat she felt the familiar kick of adrenaline as she realized she hadn't seen the post today. Maybe this would be the day that would bring Hildegarde's second letter to her door.

Mickey bounced up the stairs two at a time and let herself in. Sadly, her excited feeling petered out when she looked through the envelopes sitting on the mat and saw there was nothing for her, just a few official-looking envelopes addressed to her parents.

Mickey noticed that her parents' work shoes were missing from the hallway and realized they were still at the office. They were both scientists and kept odd hours as they oversaw important experiments and projects at their lab, so Mickey was often allowed to let herself in. This left her plenty of time for her secret animal spy work.

She made her way into the kitchen and poured herself a glass of water as she knew it was good for the brain to stay hydrated, then she flicked through the newspaper that was lying on the kitchen table. Mickey usually liked the puzzles page best, but a story with the word

'MYSTERIOUS'

in the headline immediately drew her eye.

MYSTERIOUS DISAPPEARANCE
OF COUNCIL LEADER

Concerns have been raised for retired council leader, Mrs Marjorie Leigh, who has been missing for several days. Police said, 'If anyone has any information or knows of the whereabouts of Mrs Leigh, please contact Lower Bridge Street Police Station.'

Dr Charlotte Reddick, who attends a crossword enthusiasts' circle with Mrs Leigh, spoke of her 'indomitable' nature and expressed concern for her wellbeing. 'It's not like Marjorie to disappear. She's at our crossword club every week without fail. There were rumours that she used to crack codes for a living, which makes sense because she beat us all every week.'

There was a picture of Marjorie to accompany the article. She was sitting in her house, smiling at the camera.

A puzzle solver just like Mickey. She hoped Marjorie Leigh was found safe and well soon. Mickey continued flicking through the paper and came across a second article which heightened her interest.

ESPIONAGE EVENT CANCELLED

The Book Festival on the Green regret to announce the cancellation of 'An Evening with Former Espionage Agent Samira Khan,' due to unforeseen circumstances.

A spokesperson for the festival said 'We've been looking forward to the event for months and spoke to Ms Khan last week but yesterday we received a voicemail saying she could no longer attend. We hope she'll be able to attend next year and have offered all ticket holders a full refund.'

Underneath the article was a photo of Ms Khan. She was sitting in her study, grinning at the camera, and holding up a copy of her latest book: *The Puzzler's Companion: Logic Puzzles and Crossword Conundrums to Exercise Your Brain.*

So two women, both experts at solving puzzles, had gone missing at the same time. The two articles were pages apart and no connection had been drawn between the two, which struck Mickey as odd. Were the disappearances connected? Mickey pulled the pages free and laid them side by side on the kitchen table. Both women were smiling at the camera from their living rooms. Marjorie had a mop of wild curls, Samira a neat bun. Mickey studied the backgrounds of both pictures and her heart gave a jolt. Both women were sitting in front of bookcases, and Mickey noticed a familiar flash of green sitting on the shelf. The same green on the spine of her very favourite book, *Hildegarde L. McTavish's Cracking the Codes.*

Mickey quickly rattled through the evidence in her head:

> TWO MISSING WOMEN
>
> BOTH CROSSWORD EXPERTS
>
> BOTH AROUND HILDEGARDE'S AGE
>
> BOTH HAD HILDEGARDE'S BOOK IN THEIR HOMES
>
> MS KHAN IS OPENLY A FORMER SPY
>
> THERE ARE RUMOURS THAT MRS LEIGH USED TO CRACK CODES FOR A LIVING

Mickey's brain whirred as she realized a worrisome possibility— what if they were *both* former spies, like Hildegarde, and something bad had happened to them?

And worse, if two spies had gone missing, why not three—maybe Hildegarde *really* was in trouble and that was why she hadn't been in touch!

What she needed, Mickey realized, was a way to contact Hildegarde. She looked at her letter again but, as she already knew, there was no return address. If only Hildegarde had a pet that the **COBRA** network could contact. Mickey had learned on a documentary that Hildegarde had once had a tortoise called Maura, but she had no idea if this was still the case. Tortoises can live a really long time so she supposed it was possible.

MAURA! Mickey's brain felt all fizzy as it started spotting links and connections everywhere. Astrid had previously mentioned a friend called Maura who she sometimes exchanged coded messages with which sounded promising, but she had never mentioned what kind of animal Maura was. Could Astrid's friend and Hildegarde's pet be one and the same? Mickey knew it was a long shot but it was worth a try.

Mickey looked at the clock and realized her parents would be home shortly, so instead of dashing back to **COBRA** HQ, she ran to the desk in her room, took out a sheet of writing paper, and quickly scribbled a note to Astrid asking after her code-cracking friend, Maura. Mickey quickly explained her concerns and marked the message

<u>URGENT</u>

Mickey opened the window and whistled the short tune Astrid had taught her to call a bird from the Bird-Mail service. **COBRA** communicated by b-mails, not emails, messages sent by flying birds. The good thing about this service was you never seemed to be more than a few feet from a bird, but the disadvantage was some birds got distracted and tried to eat their messages en route.

Within a few minutes of her whistle, a robin landed on the windowsill. It looked at Mickey and carefully blinked its bright eyes three times—the **COBRA** signal to identify an agent—Mickey tapped her own head three times in response and handed over her message. And just in time, as the bird flew off with her precious note to Astrid attached to its leg, Mickey heard the familiar sound of her parents' feet trudging up the stairs and the shuffle of shopping bags as they set them down out on the landing.

Mickey ran to open the door before they had to trouble themselves with trying to find the key and hoped that she'd find the key to her own mystery soon.

Chapter

5

Astrid was Mickey's closest friend in **COBRA**, and on reading Mickey's note, she had taken immediate action. She had only ever exchanged codes and puzzles via Bird-Mail with Maura and didn't even know what kind of animal she was, let alone who she lived with. However, Astrid had sent an urgent message to Maura, asking if she was *a)* a tortoise and *b)* living with Hildegarde.

The next day Astrid had received a Bird-Mail herself. 'Top Secret,' Maura had replied, 'can't leave a written record.' Astrid then suggested they meet up and made the arrangements.

So two days later, on Saturday morning, Mickey headed to the park where Astrid had arranged to meet Maura. Mickey made a beeline for the trees lining the river and heard a 'pssst'. She looked up to see Astrid hanging by her tail and waving at her. Mickey grinned and pulled herself up into the tree. Astrid scampered over to greet her.

'Are you ready?' Astrid asked.

'Never readier,' said Mickey. 'Ready for the backpack trick?'

Astrid jumped onto Mickey's back and looped her long arms around Mickey's human ones. Mickey climbed back down the tree, more carefully now she was carrying a precious load. She hoped that anyone observing her would just think she was a girl with a novelty backpack, rather than a human spy and a spider monkey secret agent.

Mickey (and the Astrid backpack) headed towards the benches that formed a circle around the fountain in the middle of the park. There were purple and white winter flowers dotted around. The fountain trickled water into the pond, the water droplets shining in the morning sun.

Mickey headed to the middle bench where they had arranged to meet Maura. She nodded to the two seagulls who had been tasked with sitting on the bench to reserve it. They had been aggressively flapping at any other person who had tried to sit there but flew off as Mickey and Astrid arrived.

Mickey settled herself down and looked at her watch.

'Two minutes to ten,' she whispered to her backpack. 'Can you see anything?'

'Not yet,' Astrid whispered back.

Mickey scanned the park looking for an animal who might be Maura. The fountain area was surrounded by long flat playing fields, so she should be able to see anyone on the approach, but all seemed quiet. Mickey's eye was drawn back to the fountain and the water running onto the rocks below.

Then she saw something odd and blinked furiously to check it was real.

'Astrid,' she hissed.

'Yes?' said the monkey, leaning up towards her ear.

'Did that rock just . . . move?'

Astrid followed Mickey's gaze. The base of the fountain had a small rockery and one of the rocks seemed to be raising itself up and down.

'That rock is moving,' said Mickey. 'Do you think that's Maura?'

Astrid peered over. 'It could be.'

Mickey looked at the rock, thoughtfully, and then she very purposefully blinked three times. And just in case Maura couldn't see her she added out loud, 'I'm blinking three times.'

Watching carefully, Mickey and Astrid

watched as a small tortoise leg appeared and
tapped the rock three times in response.

Mickey dashed towards the fountain and
looked into the water.

'Maura?' she called softly. A head appeared
as Mickey realized that Maura was indeed
the rock and found herself face to face with
a very wrinkled-looking tortoise.

'Maura!' cried Astrid, swinging down from
Mickey's back and rushing to embrace the
tortoise. 'So lovely to meet you in person at
long last!'

'I hope you don't mind getting a bit wet,' said Maura. 'I didn't mean to be mysterious, but anyone can read a letter. Whereas here, the running water is a good countermeasure should anyone be listening to what we say. I learned that trick from Hildegarde.'

'So you *do* live with Hildegarde!' exclaimed Mickey.

The tortoise nodded slowly. Mickey had never seen a tortoise look proud but the feeling radiated from Maura.

'I did, and we were happy, but a week ago she completely vanished and I'm worried she has been kidnapped. She'd been working in the study, but when I came back in to see her, the room had been ransacked and Hildegarde was gone! I just don't know where she is! I have tried searching the house for clues, but I can't move very fast, and I haven't uncovered anything that might lead me to her.'

Mickey, who was used to working with Tilda the sloth, could quite imagine how painstakingly slow Maura's search would have been.

'I was so relieved when I got your message because I thought if you were interested in Hildegarde then maybe you would be able to help me.'

'Why didn't you come to us straight away?' asked Astrid.

'I thought **COBRA** only dealt with issues affecting the animal kingdom,' said Maura. 'I didn't think you'd be interested in a People Problem.'

'That's not true! **COBRA** would help if a human was in trouble. Isn't that right, Astrid?' Mickey asked.

Mickey turned to the spider monkey for reassurance but Astrid didn't quite meet her eye.

'Does Hildegarde . . . does she know you can talk to humans?' asked Mickey gently.

'We have been friends for many years, but she doesn't know that animals can communicate with humans and vice versa if they wish to. She often talked to me as though she thought I could reply though—she always says a tortoise is an excellent sounding board.'

'She sounds wonderful,' said Astrid.

'She is!' said Mickey and Maura together.

'And if she's in trouble, we need to find her and fast,' said Mickey. 'Maura, can you take us to the house? There might be clues there.'

The tortoise nodded slowly. 'Of course.'

'I'll carry you!' said Mickey. 'So you can move around unnoticed,' she added quickly, so as not to hurt Maura's feelings.

'Quickly please,' said Maura. 'There isn't a moment to lose!'

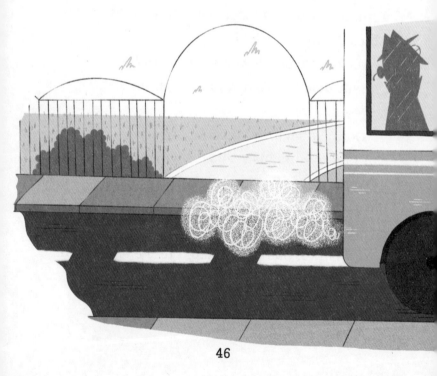

Chapter

6

Mickey carefully wiped the drops of water off Maura's shell with her sleeve then placed her inside her cotton tote bag with her woolly hat lying along the bottom to try and make it more comfortable.

'I got here via the gulls,' Maura's voice said from inside the bag. 'A few of them kindly carried me to our meeting place. But I think I can remember the way back home. We need to get what you humans like to call a "bus".'

Mickey navigated their way to the right stop and boarded the bus with Astrid on her back and Maura hidden in the bag.

They sat on the top deck and it wove its way towards the city.

After a few stops, Maura advised Mickey to get off the bus and then directed them to a beautiful old square with red-brick houses around the edge. Each stretched up several stories and they had colourful front doors and well-tended hedges.

Maura directed them to the house on the corner then pointed to a planter full of rosemary. 'The spare key is in that one. Hildegarde says that rosemary helps her memory.'

Mickey smiled as she reached down to search. She knew all about Hildegarde's love of plants and their uses. She found the key, unlocked the sage green front door, and slid the key into her pocket for safekeeping while they looked around. Then Mickey put Maura on the ground so she could lead the way into her own home.

'Please come in,' said Maura proudly as Mickey and Astrid followed her into the house.

'WOW!' Mickey exclaimed as she looked around. It was the most amazing house she had ever been in. Every inch of the hallway was stuffed with books of all sizes and other little curiosities. Mickey could see a pair of binoculars sitting on top of a stack of dictionaries, all in different languages, a golden atlas next to a globe, and a selection of sunglasses lined up neatly on the windowsill. There was a skylight directly above them which cast miniature rainbows around the room, and the floor tiles replicated a map of the world. Everything about the room screamed **ADVENTURE** and **MYSTERY** and they were still only in Hildegarde's hall. There was a large table at the end of the hall with a huge jigsaw of Venice on it showing a bridge over a canal at sunset. The jigsaw was complete apart from one piece missing from the middle. 'We couldn't find the last piece, but Hildegarde said we were not to leave a challenge uncompleted, so we're still looking,' Maura explained.

Mickey sat down on a bench next to

the front door which doubled up as a shoe rack. She pulled out the drawer underneath to reveal a large selection of shoes. They were all so different—just the sort of shoe collection you would need to pull off a variety of different disguises. There was a pair of heavy biker books, a pair of glittery high heels, and a pair of smartly polished brogues. Mickey wondered again if Hildegarde was still operating as a spy somehow and wasn't actually retired at all.

'Where do we start our search?' asked Astrid.

'Maura, what did you and Hildegarde do right before she went missing?' asked Mickey.

'She was in the study,' said Maura, as she climbed onto a small trolley in the hallway. Maura nudged a lever with her nose and the trolley rolled into action. 'Hildegarde made this for me so I could zip around the house more quickly. She said my brain works faster than my feet.'

'Oh wow, we should get one for Tilda,' said Astrid.

'It's this way!' said Maura as she zipped her way down the hall, through a door and into the study.

Mickey walked into the study and gasped in shock. Unlike the hallway, this room was in complete disarray. Papers were strewn all over the floor, the paintings were hanging at unusual angles, and the only thing that looked at all neat was the stack of books lined up on top of the mantelpiece, sitting under a tilted painting of some sunflowers. The desk was covered with papers but most of them were covered in a lake of dried blue ink which had spilled out from an inkwell that was lying on its side. Mickey saw a copy of *Cracking the Codes* sitting just outside of the big spill and instinctively picked it up and held it close to her.

'What do you think happened here?' Mickey asked.

'I don't know!' said Maura sadly. 'I was in the garden and when I came back inside the house, Hildegarde was gone and the study looked like this. It's almost like . . .'

Suddenly there was a loud

SMASH!!!

sound which
filled the room.

'What was that?' asked Astrid.

'It came from the back of the house!' said Maura. 'Maybe whoever took Hildegarde has come back for something else?'

Mickey listened carefully and heard the unmistakable sound of someone clearing their throat, followed by heavy footsteps. They were getting louder and seemed to be heading towards the study where they were! She wanted to stay and investigate, but she knew she had to get Maura and Astrid to safety, so she made a quick decision.

'Quick!' she cried. 'The window!'

With a leap, Astrid was at the window. She expertly worked the catch and pushed it open—Mickey grabbed Maura and leapt through, followed by Astrid who pulled the window closed behind them. Then, Astrid jumped onto Mickey's back and Mickey ran as fast as she could. Her heart was hammering in her chest and she once again thanked her lucky stars she had worked so hard at gymnastics as she vaulted Hildegarde's fence and dashed away, putting as much distance between herself and the house as possible before stopping to catch her breath.

'I think Hildegarde must be in real trouble,' said Mickey seriously. 'She may have been kidnapped. The intruder just now may be looking for something they didn't get the first time around, or there's another criminal on the loose!'

'This is terrible, she must be in real danger,' cried Maura. 'We need to find her!'

Mickey quite agreed. Her hero and master spy extraordinaire was in trouble, and Mickey would do anything to get her back!

Chapter

It was only later that Mickey realized she was still clutching Hildegarde's copy of *Cracking the Codes* from her study.

'Did anyone catch a glimpse of the intruder?' Mickey asked as they walked quickly back to the bus stop.

'I didn't, I was too busy trying to get the window open,' said Astrid. 'Maura? Did you see anything?'

'Not really,' came Maura's voice from the tote bag. 'I didn't have a clear view, but from the sound of the footsteps I would estimate they were very tall, at least as tall as a table and almost definitely human.'

This, thought Mickey, was exactly why **COBRA** needed a Human Liaison Officer. The animals didn't always notice the

same details about humans that Mickey could spot. She just wished she'd been able to catch a glimpse of the mystery intruder as they'd fled from Hildegarde's house.

'This is exactly why we don't deal with problems concerning humans,' said Coby when Mickey, Astrid, and Maura had breathlessly updated the High Committee on Hildegarde's disappearance and their lucky escape, back at **COBRA** HQ. 'We are an animal-led organization and that is where our focus should be. This morning's mission put you, Astrid, and Maura in real danger. It just proves that human-based missions are not worth the risk.'

Mickey was so worried about Hildegarde she found the courage to do something she would never normally dare to: she disagreed with Coby.

'But *I'M* a human,' she pointed out.

'And whose fault is that?' asked Clarke, swishing his tail.

'Clarke, please remember your manners,' interrupted Rupert.

'But you *do* have some interaction with the human world when you need it for your cases,' said Mickey desperately. 'Hildegarde's disappearance is important to me because I want to make sure she's okay, but it affects the animal world too. Maura at the very least! AND, Hildegarde was a secret agent, so her going missing could put the security of the country at risk and then that would affect everyone who lives here—human and animal! You can't say it doesn't affect animals just because it doesn't affect them *yet*. AND I've worked on two missions for you, and have been loyal and brave. I have proved myself and now I need you to help me.' Mickey took a deep breath and felt the air flow back into her lungs after her speech. She looked at Coby who had her head tilted to one side, her neck hood flaring as she considered Mickey's words.

'I can see your position,' she said calmly. 'And if it was just up to me, I would probably answer differently. But I am responsible for **COBRA**, its High Committee and all the animals we have sworn to protect. Taking on tasks that edge us into the human world when an animal is in danger makes the risk tolerable. Charging into a human problem that could endanger animals—we always worry about exposure—with only humans at stake—it's too much of a risk.'

'I have to investigate. I would prefer to do it as part of **COBRA**, but if you won't help me, I'll have to do it alone.' Mickey folded her arms. She could not back down on this one. Not when Hildegarde was in danger.

'Mickey,' said Coby gently. 'I understand your position. But you also need to understand that I have a commitment to honour our members who run calculated risks for **COBRA** all the time and did not sign up to take on these additional dangers.'

Tilda slowly lifted one arm into the air.

'Don't worry Tilda,' said Coby quickly,

'you won't have to do anything you are uncomfortable with; it's part of **COBRA**'s mission to stay secret and to shield our existence and we will continue to do so.'

'It's not that,' said the sloth. Mickey, Coby and the rest of the High Committee turned to Tilda who was rarely the first one to speak or give an opinion in meetings. 'Actually, I'd . . . I'd like to help Mickey. And Hildegarde. And Maura.'

'Reallllllly?' said Coby.

Tilda leaned forward in her seat. 'Yes, I think we *should* help. It's the right thing to do.'

Coby swivelled in a figure of eight. 'I suppose . . . we could help in principle . . . but we can't expect the assistance of any other animals outside of the **COBRA** High Committee. Hildegarde's safety may be at risk, but I can't risk my agents on the ground. Do you understand?'

'Understood,' said Mickey quickly. 'I would never want anyone to do something they felt uncomfortable with. I've just never done a mission on my own and I'd rather do it with the team, our team, the best team.'

'I'm in,' said Astrid, holding two long limbs in the air. 'For you, and for Maura.'

'After all your brilliant work with **COBRA**, it would be remiss of me if I did not also offer my place by your side, my dear,' said Rupert, sliding down the table to stand near Mickey.

'Clarke?' asked Mickey. 'It wouldn't be the same without you.'

The cat looked around the room, rolled his eyes and said, 'Well, I can't let you go on a mission without me, it would be a disaster. What do we do next?'

Mickey smiled. 'We get to work—Operation Missing Spy is

GO!'

Chapter

8

Mickey set to work, building
a giant wall of Post-it notes
in front of their meeting table
so everyone could see all the
information they had gathered
so far, including the newspaper
articles about the two missing
women, Samira and Marjorie.

Hildegarde's own copy of *Cracking the Codes* was on the desk in front of her, making her feel braver about commandeering **COBRA** HQ for a mission she wasn't one hundred per cent certain Coby approved of.

'Where do you want to begin?' asked the snake, giving her a nod.

'At the beginning,' said Mickey. 'We should retrace Hildegarde's last steps, and luckily we have a star witness in Maura.'

'I was wondering about that,' said Coby. 'If Hildegarde is such a super spy, then why did she never realize that Maura could talk?'

'Because I kept it from her,' replied Maura. 'Hildegarde has no idea! Though I think she'd love to know. She'd be tickled to think there was one huge secret in her own house that she was unaware of!'

'But humans do talk to their pets sometimes and might air their worries out loud. Did she say anything that now seems suspicious?' asked Mickey. 'Perhaps you could cast your mind back to the day she disappeared?'

'Just run us through what you can remember,' said Tilda, getting ready to take notes.

'I'm sorry, I don't think I'll be much use here,' said Maura. 'It was a very normal day. I was out in the garden, Hildegarde was working in her study with the door closed and, well, when I went to check on her she was gone and the room had been ransacked.'

'Didn't you hear anything?' asked Clarke, tilting his head to one side. 'Nothing suspicious at all?'

'I was inside my shell,' said Maura. 'I didn't know I needed to be on alert, and believe me, I feel awful about it now. If I'd been in the house I might have seen what happened to her. Oh dear!'

Astrid reached out a paw to comfort the tortoise. 'It wasn't your fault at all, and you're doing everything you can to help now, aren't you?'

Maura nodded. 'I'm just so worried about her.'

'We need to think about it logically,' said

Mickey. 'Can we ask the birds to keep a look out for Hildegarde or see if any of the local birds saw anything suspicious since she went missing? Or, one of them might have a description of the person who broke into the house while we were there, that could be really useful!'

The animals, even Astrid, shifted in their seats. 'I don't think we can do that, my dear,' said Rupert.

'No,' said Coby more sharply. 'I told you that if we are to take on this mission, we mustn't drag other animals into it. Besides, this human of yours is likely to be in a human place or building, so the animals will be of little help.'

'Agreed,' said Rupert. 'What if Hildegarde just fancied some time alone?'

'Maybe she's at the shops?' said Astrid.

'For a whole week?' asked Mickey. 'And why was the house such a mess?'

'Some creatures quite like a mess,' said Rupert, moving his tail to cover up the crumbs scattered around his paws.

Mickey forced herself to breathe slowly and tried to stay calm. The animals would be taking this much more seriously if it was an animal who had gone missing, and she was running out of ways to try and convince them. Her eyes landed on Hildegarde's book in front of her, and out of habit she picked it up and flicked through the pages for comfort. She had read the book so many times it felt like greeting an old friend. Then her eye caught something at the beginning of one of the chapters. It was an illustration of one of Hildegarde's quotes:

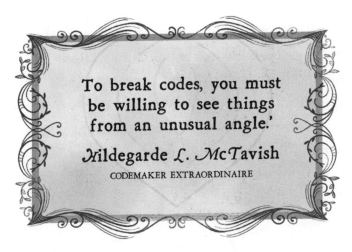

'To break codes, you must be willing to see things from an unusual angle.'

Hildegarde L. McTavish

CODEMAKER EXTRAORDINAIRE

There was a symbol hand-drawn around the quote! Mickey turned the page upside down and realized that it looked an awful lot like the flame of a candle. Remembering that Hildegarde was a big fan of the type of invisible ink which only revealed itself when heat was applied, Mickey looked around the room quickly.

'Does anyone have a hairdryer?' As she looked at their surprised faces, she quickly remembered who she was talking to. 'Or any kind of heat source?'

'Perhaps the lamp?' asked Rupert gesturing towards it.

'Great idea!' said Mickey. She pressed that page of the book to the bulb and waited, hoping it would work and show that her hunch was correct.

When she turned the book the right way around there were new symbols on the page.

'I think Hildegarde has left a message!' said Mickey. 'It's a spiral code!'

L	O	O	K	C	L
N	T	I	N	G	O
I	O	W	E	O	S
A	L	S	R	F	E
P	F	N	U	S	L
E	H	T	T	A	Y

Mickey had come across spiral codes before. You began in the top left corner then followed the message along the line, then down and around in a spiral to reveal the secret:

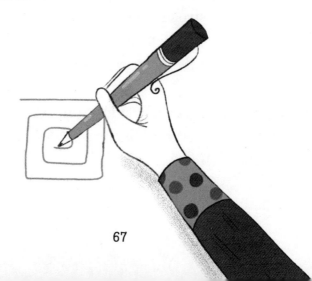

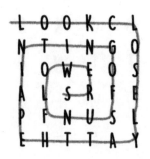

'Look,' said Mickey. 'It says

"LOOK CLOSELY AT THE PAINTING OF SUNFLOWERS".'

'A painting of some flowers?' said Clarke. 'I doubt that will help us; it's incredibly vague!'

'You know nothing of art,' said Rupert. 'The brushstrokes, the passion. It could be a clue to her state of mind, it could be the key to an elaborate mystery crossing continents or . . .'

'A painting in our study,' said Maura suddenly. 'We have this picture! Perhaps there's a clue there!'

Chapter

9

The next morning, Mickey found herself
hovering outside Hildegarde's house once
again, using the spare key to open her front
door and cautiously enter.

'Hello?' she called out, remembering with
a shiver the sound of breaking glass and
heavy footsteps from the day before. 'Can
you hear anything?' she whispered to Clarke

and Rupert who were accompanying her. It had been agreed that a rat and a cat were the least suspicious if they came across any other humans.

'I can't hear anyone,' said Clarke, tipping his head from side to side.

Rupert sniffed the air. 'It all seems clear to me too. I think we're safe to enter.'

Mickey crept into the hall and retraced her steps down the hallway to Hildegarde's study. There was the mantelpiece topped with its neat stack of books that she had seen before, and there was the giant painting of sunflowers hanging above the fireplace at a funny angle. Mickey looked at the painting. It was full of jolly colours, but she couldn't see any letters, numbers, or anything that looked like a code. If there were clues hidden inside the painting, they were proving very elusive indeed.

Mickey stepped back and looked at the painting again.

'Sunflowers, sunflowers, oh *sunflowers!*' she cried as her eyes noticed the title of one of the books on the mantelpiece. The spine was a golden orange and in bold black type the title read *A History of Sunflowers*. Mickey quickly scanned the rest of the books and saw that hidden between *101 Ways with a Wig, How to Read Minds and Influence People,* and *Disguising your Way out of Danger* there was one more—*Sam's Sunflowers*—and then, she spotted yet another one—*Towards the Sun, Flowers will Grow: A Collection of Nature Verses*.

'There are three books about sunflowers, below a painting of them. Maybe that's the trick?' Mickey pondered aloud.

'Seems quite possible, my dear,' said Rupert. 'But the trick to what?'

'I detest sunflower seeds,' said Clarke. 'They get stuck in your teeth.'

Mickey reached out to pull *Sam's Sunflowers* down for a closer look, but the book stuck firm. She tried wriggling it. Still nothing.

'I wonder . . .' she murmured, as instead of pulling the book, she tried pushing it towards the wall. It slid forwards an inch. 'Interesting,' she said, finding the other two sunflower books and pushing them in to match. Once all three were in place, there was a smart click and the wall juddered. Mickey gave it a hefty shove and it flew open, revealing a mirror image of the room they were currently in. The same mirror on the opposite wall, the same walnut desk covered in papers but without the spilled ink, and crucially, sitting at the desk, was Mickey's hero—*Hildegarde Louise McTavish*.

She looked straight at Mickey and frowned. Mickey's heart sank. Was Hildegarde about to prove herself to be friend or foe?

Chapter
10

Hildegarde looked at Mickey, Clarke, and Rupert with an undecipherable expression on her face, but then she smiled and her whole face lit up.

'Well, I don't believe it. Mickey? Is that you?'

Mickey had planned over and over all the things she would say when she finally got to meet Hildegarde, but in that moment, her usually quick brain betrayed her, and all that came out was a small squeak.

Hildegarde smiled and placed the book she had been reading on her desk. 'I *am* impressed that you figured it out. You are a better spy than I thought. For someone working alone, I would go so far as to say you are exceptional.' Mickey beamed and felt Clarke bristle behind her.

'Welcome to my secret study,' Hildegarde continued, 'the one where I can retreat to in times of trouble. However, I make sure to leave clues so those who may really need me know how to find me.'

'What sort of trouble are you in?' Mickey asked.

'I fear someone has been trying to break into the house, so I thought I'd get there first. I staged my own break-in! If someone is after you, it's best to make it look like someone else got there first, makes them give up faster. But I left the coded message so if someone really needed me they would know where to look.'

'Do you know what the intruders are looking for?' asked Mickey.

'I'm afraid I think it is me,' said Hildegarde sadly, 'though I'm still trying to work out *who* and *why*. That's why I took precautions and retreated to my secure bunker. It's no huge hardship—I have my books—though I regret not being able to find Maura in my haste.'

'I'm sure she's okay,' said Mickey. 'Tortoises are quite hardy; after all, they've got their homes on their back at any time.'

'Very true, very true,' said Hildegarde. 'And are these your pets?' she asked, gesturing to Clarke and Rupert.

Mickey's brain was working quickly. On the one hand, she could hear Coby's dire warnings that **COBRA** activities must stay secret, but on the other, she knew her spy skills had only been sharpened and enhanced by working for **COBRA** and she didn't want to take all the credit herself. She decided to test the water and see how Hildegarde reacted to the idea of animal spies.

'They are my pets . . . and also spies themselves!' she said. Rupert's eyes widened while Clarke scowled, but both animals kept their gazes directed straight at Hildegarde to see what she would do next.

'Animal spies . . .' said Hildegarde, bending down slowly to their level. 'They are lovely pets. It's unusual you refer to them as fellow agents, but all the greatest code-crackers have their quirks.' Hildegarde paused, then her face lit up as she had a new thought. 'My friend Marjorie had a fox that used to follow her around, and was it Louis Carter who had the house full of parrots? Very intelligent animals you know. There was one called Alex who learned over a hundred words. Not great for a spy, mind you. What if they repeated your secrets? Perhaps that's why Lou always wound up in the most awful scrapes. Anyway, your pets are just delightful. Here kitty,' she called to Clarke, patting her leg to try and entice him over to her. Mickey gave him a *look* but he huffed and turned to face the wall instead.

'They really do help,' said Mickey trying to explain, but Hildegarde cut her off and held out a hand.

'Oh, you don't need to explain, I'm a huge animal lover as well. So often, when I was stuck on a problem, I would just chat it all out to Maura, my tortoise. And would you believe it, it almost seemed like she knew what I was saying!'

Oh, Mickey was quite sure Maura had understood every word as she'd had that conversation herself, but she couldn't tell Hildegarde the full story without risking the wrath of Coby, so instead she forced herself to smile back and nod her head.

'Does the cat liked to be petted?' asked Hildegarde, moving towards Clarke, who Mickey could see was looking most offended. She dived over to pick him up first and Clarke hissed.

'Sorry,' she said, 'he's a bit unsure of strangers.'

'And I imagine I seem stranger than most,' said Hildegarde as a cuckoo clock chimed in the corner, and Mickey saw what looked like an alarm clock with wings attached jumping out on a spring.

'A little joke, you know,' said Hildegarde, following her eyeline. 'Time flies and all that.' She paused to watch the clock flutter around then turned back to look at Rupert.

'Is this the same rat that you rescued from the Impossible Vault or do you have a whole mischief of them?'

Mickey gulped. She wasn't sure how much of the events down inside the Impossible Vault Hildegarde was aware of.

'How did you know I was in the vault?' asked Mickey, desperate to know the answer to a question that had been at the back of her mind ever since she'd first received Hildegarde's letter.

'Oh, from Robert,' said Hildegarde. 'He was the guard on duty that day, an old friend. He's a great animal lover, you'd like him, and he's particularly fond of cats.' Mickey tried not to look directly at Clarke who had been the one to distract Robert the day they broke into the bank.

'Yes, he didn't say anything officially as he was terribly embarrassed that you had managed to slip past him. He caught a glimpse of you on the feed but then was apparently distracted by a cat and didn't think anything of it until he found a door open that shouldn't have been and checked the tapes. As nothing was taken, he didn't take it any further but felt that I should know someone had worked out how to break into my vault—it's never happened before, you know.

'But I'm also terribly impressed you tracked me down, my dear, and working alone makes it all the more impressive.'

'I loved your letter, and I was waiting patiently,' Mickey said, keen to explain her actions. 'I began to worry that you were in trouble so I tracked down your address. And it wasn't just you I was worried about. I think something strange may be happening to other, "retired" spies.'

'Really?' said Hildegarde. 'I'm all ears. Will you stay for lunch?' Hildegarde herded Mickey towards the kitchen. Rupert and Clarke followed closely behind at the promise of food.

'Something to drink?' asked Hildegarde, as she bustled around the room. 'Gunpowder green tea? My special ginger drink? Coffee made from elephant dung?'

'Just a squash, please,' said Mickey.

'Coming up,' said Hildegarde, pouring out a glass then searching through the cupboards for ingredients and pouring water into a pan to cook a pile of pasta.

Mickey watched her move around in awe. After all the years she'd read her books and dreamed of meeting Hildegarde, here she was in front of her, cooking pasta—it was quite surreal.

I think spies are going missing.'

Mickey pulled the newspaper articles from

her pocket and laid them out on the table.

Hildegarde came over and peered at the articles through her specs. 'Marjorie?' she murmured. 'Oh, what have you done now? And Samira. My, my . . . but what do you know about this?'

'Do you know these women?' asked Mickey. 'They're both missing and I think they both used to be spies. It says that Samira gives talks about being an ex-agent but there were rumours that Marjorie might have been one too.'

'Well, obviously, I can neither confirm nor deny that,' said Hildegarde briskly. 'Official secrets and all that.'

'But you said Marjorie,' said Mickey. 'Didn't you mention her earlier? The one who had the fox?'

'Hmmm,' said Hildegarde. 'MAYBE. Well, let's play with your theory—throw it in the air and see what sticks. It's like cooking pasta—' She leapt to the stove and ladled some out of the water. 'You throw it at the wall.' Hildegarde paused to lob a bit of the spaghetti straight at the wall behind Mickey. Some slid to the ground, but a couple of strands stuck fast. 'Excellent! The pasta sticks and so might your theory—are you ready to eat?'

Mickey nodded. Solving a mystery with her hero? Wild horses couldn't drag her away.

Chapter

11

Luckily, there were no wild horses in sight,
but Mickey did have an undercover cat and
rat leaning against her legs to remind her
that they would quite like to eat too. Mickey
knew Clarke would be cross that he didn't
have a place set at the table, and Rupert
would be considering it a social faux pas not
to ensure *all* your guests were fed. Luckily,
Hildegarde made a similar observation
herself.

'Are the pets hungry?' she asked as she
ladled out two huge bowls for Mickey and
herself. Clarke had suddenly decided he might
be affectionate after all and was coming
towards Hildegarde's legs in full pet cat mode
now there was food on offer.

'Here you go,' Hildegarde sang as she set
down a plate each for Rupert and Clarke.
Rupert dived straight into his bowl and began
eating noisily.

'You see Mickey,' said Hildegarde as she
played with her fork, 'what you won't know,
because it isn't in any of my books, is this.'

She paused to draw breath and Mickey
saw Clarke tip his ear in their direction and

84

Rupert lean closer to them in a very obvious fashion. She gestured to them to play it cool.

'I was actually one of five founding members of this country's most secret spy organization '**The Espionage Agency**' or TEA for short, along with Samira Khan, Marjorie Leigh and two other agents named Thomasina Moore and Patrick Whitston,' said Hildegarde. 'They called us the Original Five. If Samira and Marjorie are missing and I was right to suspect that someone was also after me, then I think we need to check in on Thomasina and Patrick—they could be in grave danger. Is your pasta okay?'

'Delicious,' said Mickey. Hildegarde nodded like an approving chef on a television cookery programme then continued her story.

'The identities of the Original Five are supposed to be a closely guarded secret, but it sounds like someone knows who shouldn't. There used to be a folder containing our details but that was destroyed years ago . . . unless, of course, it wasn't and has now fallen into the wrong hands.'

'What sort of folder?' asked Mickey.

Hildegarde rummaged through a pile of cookbooks on the table and drew out a cream-coloured folder with TOP SECRET printed neatly along the top.

'I keep my secret recipes in this now, but we used to use these for our most classified documents.'

Mickey was staring at the folder. She'd definitely seen one like it before, but it had been in much worse condition and had turned yellow with age.

'Harry!' she gasped as the missing piece of the puzzle fell into place in her mind.

'Who?' asked Hildegarde.

'He's the one who was trying to break into The Impossible Vault,' said Mickey. 'We—I mean I—' she quickly corrected herself to protect **COBRA**'s role in their last adventure, 'confronted a thief called Harry in a bank vault. He was the one who tricked us, I mean me, into getting there because I had to rescue Rupert. He left the valuable jewels and gold in the vault but escaped with a folder that looked just like that one.'

Hildegarde groaned. 'So it may have fallen into the wrong hands. This means that someone out there knows we used to work together, and how to track us all down.'

'But what use would the files be all these years later?' asked Mickey. 'It must have been important enough for Harry to want to get into The Impossible Vault, but aren't you all retired now?'

'A spy is never truly retired,' said Hildegarde with a twinkle in her eye. 'But the identity of **The Espionage Agency**'s founders has never been made public. My current theory is this thief you encountered in the vaults—Harry, you say his name is?—has a plan of using them to blow the cover of **The Espionage Agency**, making it impossible for them to continue operating, to use the threat of blowing their cover to make some other demands, or to embarrass the current Agency by showing they can be outwitted.'

'We have to stop him!' said Mickey who had faced Harry twice before.

'That's the spirit,' said Hildegarde with a twinkle in her eye.

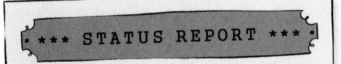

* * * STATUS REPORT * * *

[THE ORIGINAL FIVE]

HILDEGARDE L. MCTAVISH
Status: Attempted attack made but thwarted thanks to her secret study

SAMIRA KHAN
Status: Officially Missing

MARJORIE LEIGH
Status: Officially Missing

THOMASINA MOORE
Status: Unknown

PATRICK WHITSTON
Status: Unknown

Chapter

12

'If Thomasina and Patrick are safe and well, then all we will have wasted is the petrol to get to them,' said Hildegarde. 'But if our hunch is correct and this Harry has been watching their movements and taken them, then we can hunt for clues to track them down and find where Harry is keeping the others too. Come on, I'll drive.'

Hildegarde was searching for her car keys, as Mickey gestured to Clarke. 'Pssst, Clarke.' The cat looked at her with a hard stare.

'What?' he asked pointedly.

'Clarke, I know we're not supposed to be sending Bird-Mail but this is an

EMERGENCY!

Please send a message to the others to let them know there are other spies potentially missing too,' Mickey whispered.

The cat looked rebellious and turned up his nose.

'I'll sneak you something tasty if you do . . .' Mickey tempted him, knowing he had enjoyed both Hildegarde's cooking and the range of interesting smells in her kitchen.

'*Two* tasty things,' bargained Clarke.

'Done,' said Mickey.

'*Fiiiine*,' sighed Clarke before shooting out of the kitchen in a cat-shaped blur.

'Oh, where's the kitty cat?' asked Hildegarde, coming back in to the kitchen holding her car keys.

'He's gone outside, you know what cats are like. I'm sure he'll be back in a minute.'

'Independent spirits, so marvellous!' said

Hildegarde. 'Do you know, his independence reminds me of my friend Bertha. She's marvellous—a retired agent who knits coded messages and keeps a troupe of llamas on her farm. They all go for long walks together, including through the town.'

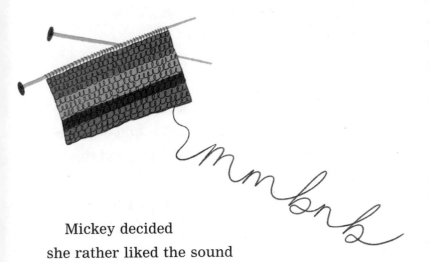

Mickey decided she rather liked the sound of Bertha.

'Shall we get going? I'm sure your rat will be okay here by himself. Let me just get him some water.' Hildegarde grabbed a saucer, filled it with water then put it down next to three identical saucers which didn't contain water. 'A little challenge for your creatures; it is good to keep their brains stimulated, you know.'

Rupert looked up at Mickey who knew just how stimulated the brains of her 'pets' truly were. She felt a wave of guilt envelop her at the idea of leaving them out.

'Can't they come too?' asked Mickey. 'I work best with my team.'

'Well,' said Hildegarde, trying to be kind, 'one does admire quirkiness in an agent, but action in the field is no place for a pet. And this mission will be a doddle for you—you've done so much by yourself already, and this time we'll be a team of two!'

Mickey couldn't bear it any longer.

'But I already work in a team,' she confessed. 'It's a secret group of animal spies called **COBRA**. This is Rupert, he's the head of Wild Animals, and he's really quite senior.'

'I seeeee,' said Hildegarde, seemingly lost for words for the first time.

'It's true,' said Mickey seriously. 'We've dealt with Harry before so I think we can help this time too. But, **COBRA** is supposed to be secret—the human world mustn't know about them. Coby will be so cross when she finds out I've told you, but I trust you, and people are in danger, so I think you need to know all the facts. I think if you work with **COBRA** we can crack this case together.'

She paused to catch her breath as Hildegarde looked between her and Rupert very carefully.

'This Coby would be . . . angry?' she asked. 'You mean you've found a way to communicate with animals? How? Sign language? I know that's been tried before with limited success.' Hildegarde tried waving at Rupert then called 'Hello Mr Rat' loudly, but Rupert just wrinkled his nose in response.

'He really *can* talk,' said Mickey desperately. Rupert shot her a worried look.

'Oh dear, perhaps there was something wrong with the food,' said Hildegarde, looking around the kitchen. She put a hand to Mickey's forehead then to her own. 'You do feel quite well though? How many fingers can you see?' She held up three fingers on her left hand.

'Animals *can* talk to humans,' Mickey persisted. 'They just . . . choose not to most of the time. Tell her, Rupert! It's okay, in fact, it's the polite thing to do.' Mickey added the last part because she knew how much the rat prided himself on his manners.

Time slowed down as Mickey looked at Rupert, willing him to prove to her hero that she was telling the truth. However, he kept his mouth firmly closed and Mickey's heart sank as she realized he wasn't going to speak.

'Well?' asked Hildegarde.

Chapter

13

'Well, how do you do,' said Rupert finally. 'My name is Rupert. Delighted to make your acquaintance.'

'Oh my!!' cried Hildegarde, looking as happy as someone who had had twenty Christmases come at once. 'He really does speak! And this isn't a trick? There are no hidden cameras? How absolutely marvellous!' Hildegarde suddenly looked many years younger.

'Please don't tell anyone,' said Mickey quickly. 'Humans aren't supposed to know about **COBRA**, but I think we need both humans and animals to unite this time, if we are to have any hope of stopping Harry. Can you keep **COBRA** a secret?'

Mickey knew how much depended on Hildegarde's silence. If she wasn't able to protect **COBRA** from being exposed then Coby would never forgive her, and worst of all, Mickey might have put her friends in **COBRA** at risk.

'Of course,' said Hildegarde as Mickey breathed out in relief. 'Keeping secrets is my specialist skill!'

'I'm sorry if you thought I'd done it all by myself,' said Mickey. 'I didn't want to disappoint you.'

'Disappoint me?' said Hildegarde looking confused. 'If anything I am even *more* impressed. The best spies I know all work well in a team.'

Mickey felt herself blushing with pride and relief that Hildegarde understood. However,

the moment was interrupted by Clarke
sashaying back into the room.

'Hello, Mr Cat,' said Hildegarde. 'What do
you have to say for yourself?'

Clarke shot Mickey a furious look.

'It's okay Clarke, I trust Hildegarde to keep
our secret,' Mickey said.

'Me too,' said Rupert.

'And I take full responsibility if Coby is
cross,' Mickey added, nervously.

'On your head be it,' snarled Clarke.

Hildegarde hopped in delight at hearing
him speak.'Oh, this is just so exciting! This
could change everything—a whole network

of spying we didn't even know about—what a thrill! Wait, does this mean that Maura, my tortoise, can speak too?'

'Of course, she can,' said Clarke rolling his eyes. 'Aren't you supposed to be clever?'

'Oh the sass, I just love him,' said Hildegarde. 'He is exactly how I imagined a cat would be if they could talk, the grumpy little sausage.'

'This is Clarke,' said Mickey. 'He's one of **COBRA**'s most valuable agents.'

Hildegarde gave him a smart nod. 'Then I am most pleased to make your acquaintance, sir.'

Clarke nodded in a curt but dignified way, but Mickey knew he was thrilled at being addressed more respectfully.

'Perhaps we should introduce Hildegarde to Coby and the other **COBRA** members before we check on Thomasina and Patrick,' Mickey suggested.

'Excellent, and what kind of creature is Coby?' asked Hildegarde as they prepared to leave. 'A lizard? A bird? A bunny?'

'She's a cobra,' said Clarke, 'and she's going to be absolutely furious when she finds out what Mickey's done. I hope there are snacks as I can't *wait* to watch.'

Mickey felt a wave of anxiety crash over her. She was fairly confident that she had done the right thing, but she wasn't sure if Coby was going to see things quite the same way.

Chapter

14

After a short trip in Hildegarde's Volkswagen Beetle, which she informed them was called Ms Mildred, Mickey found herself outside **COBRA** HQ with Hildegarde, Rupert, and Clarke in tow.

'Come on, it's in here,' she said, showing Hildegarde into the entrance shed, Clarke

and Rupert trailing behind them. Mickey
approached the goldfish bowl on the desk
and tapped her head three times, which was
the trick to gaining entry. However, instead
of nodding back, the goldfish turned three
somersaults.

'I've never seen it do that before,' Mickey
murmured. Before she had a chance to ask
Rupert what it meant, the secret wall swung
open and Bertie came charging towards them
at full speed, scooped up Mickey, Clarke, and

Rupert onto his back, dashed back through the opening, and slammed it shut with his foot, leaving Hildegarde on the other side.

'Bertie? What are you doing?' asked Mickey dizzily.

'The fish said a strange woman had kidnapped you and was trying to force entry!' cried Bertie. 'Don't worry, you're safe now!'

'Excellent work, Bertie,' came Coby's voice, as she slid down the corridor. 'Thank you for dealing with this situation so quickly.' Bertie's jaw dropped wide open at getting praise from Coby herself. Mickey patted one of his long legs. 'Good job,' she whispered, as pleased for him as she was about her quick 'rescue'.

'I heard the alarm was activated,' Coby continued. 'Rupert, Clarke, Mickey, are you alright?'

Before they could answer Mickey heard the sound of Hildegarde tapping on the other side of the wall. 'Helloooo? Mickey? Was that a giraffe I just saw? Is he part of the gang too? How splendid!'

'Explain yoursssssselvessssss,'

hissed Coby. 'We got the Bird-Mail saying more human spies were missing, then you turn up here with a stranger? What is going on?'

'I had nothing to do with it,' said Clarke, stepping neatly away to one side. 'It was all Mickey.'

Thanks a bunch, Clarke, Mickey thought.

'Bertie, can I also commend you on your excellent reactions,' Mickey began, remembering the giraffe's dream of becoming an agent one day. 'It's not a kidnapper—it's Hildegarde herself, Coby, and she needs our help!'

'That may be the case,' said the snake, 'but why is she outside *my* headquarters talking about *my* Top Secret organization which she should know absolutely NOTHING about?'

'Coby, I had to tell her,' said Mickey, standing her ground. 'It's Harry. He's up to his old tricks again. He has kidnapped two, possibly even four, human spies, and we think he broke into Hildegarde's house to try to get to her as well. We don't know what he wants, but we know he is dangerous and we have to stop him. **COBRA** are the only ones who know enough about Harry to crack this case, and we need Hildegarde to help brief us on the missing spies. Don't you think it would be good to have access to human intelligence files occasionally? She wants to help us, Coby, please let her.'

'I don't think so,' said Coby.

'At least meet her?' said Mickey. 'She's just on the other side of that wall. You wouldn't have to go far—aren't you even a little bit curious? And I know you'd like to stop Harry . . .'

The snake paused to think about this. 'Fine,' Coby said, 'but she can't come inside the HQ. Let's go through into the shed.'

Bertie triggered the mechanism, and Coby led Mickey and the High Committee into the shed where they packed in, facing Hildegarde, who took being confronted by a range of animals in her stride. Last of all came Maura, who crawled forward and gently tapped Hildegarde's foot with hers.

'Maura!' said Hildegarde, picking her up. 'Have you really been able to speak all this time?'

'Yes!' said Maura.

'After all these years!'

'All these years indeed!'

Mickey saw Coby watching their exchange and hoped this clear demonstration of affection between human and animal might begin to break down Coby's reluctance to work with Hildegarde.

'And you must be Coby,' said Hildegarde politely, bowing her head.

'Yesssss,' said Coby, drawing herself up to

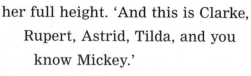

her full height. 'And this is Clarke, Rupert, Astrid, Tilda, and you know Mickey.'

'And the giraffe?' Hildegarde asked.

'Bertie,' said Mickey.

'How simply extraordinary,' said Hildegarde. 'I must commend you for your expert running of this organization. I've worked for the most advanced top secret organizations in the world, and I must say that yours is completely below the radar. It's very impressive.'

Coby nodded her head, acknowledging the praise.

'I understand you've had dealings with Harry before, is that correct?'

'Unfortunately, yes,' sighed Astrid.

'Harry,' said Coby, 'was our previous Human Liaison Officer. He is a prime example of why we do not engage with the human world, with the exception of Mickey, who has proved quite useful. Aside from bringing you here today, which I'm far from convinced was the correct thing to do.'

'You can trust me,' said Hildegarde. 'I want him stopped as much as you do. He has kidnapped two of my colleagues and may have kidnapped two more for all we know. Do you have a photo of Harry so I know exactly who we are looking for?'

'We have his whole personnel file,' said Tilda.

'His *confidential* personnel file,' whispered Astrid.

'You could just show the front page?' suggested Rupert.

Tilda went to get the file and everyone waited, anxiously looking at the floor and not quite making eye contact for the extended, extremely uncomfortable silence until the sloth crawled back into the room, Harry's personnel file in hand.

'Here it is,' she said, holding it up to Hildegarde.

Hildegarde looked at it, frowned, put on her reading glasses and peered at it again.

Harry Raynott

COBRA PERSONNEL FILE

HARRY RAYNOTT — HUMAN

EX HUMAN LIASION OFFICER

BANISHED ON COBY'S ORDERS

'Harry *Raynott*?' she exclaimed.

'You *know* him?' asked Mickey.

'Yes, I never forget a face. He once attended an interview at **The Espionage Agency** with me and the rest of the Original Five, but we didn't think he had the right skills or aptitude so passed him over. I wonder if he is trying to take his revenge on the team who turned him down?'

'Interessssting,' said Coby. 'A common enemy. Perhaps we can work together after all.'

'**COBRA** have managed to stop him twice before. I think we can do it again, especially with Hildegarde on board—he causes problems for both the human and the animal world, so let's stop him once and for all,' Mickey said, determinedly.

'And,' said Hildegarde, 'if we share resources we can cover more ground.'

'Let's form two teams,' said Coby, taking charge. 'One to check on Patrick, one to check on Thomasina. Those remaining can start going through the file we have on Harry in detail to see if there's anything in there we have missed. It's time we put a stop to his antics.'

'Perfect,' said Hildegarde. 'Mickey, I want you with me!'

Mickey beamed with pride.

Chapter

15

Mickey, Hildegarde, and Astrid were soon in the car, zooming down the road in search of Thomasina, Hildegarde keeping up a running commentary of stories while she was at the wheel, with Mickey and Astrid hanging on her every word.

'Of course, the time I really had to use my skills was when I was captured at a seaside resort. I do love the sea, don't you? Sand is so interesting. Anyway, unbeknownst to me, the enemy were in the water, and when I looked out to sea, suddenly I found myself being whisked offshore. Luckily, I gave them the slip, but it took me several hours to swim all the way back, and when I got there my friends asked me where I'd been and I had to say I'd been looking for an ice cream, and they had no idea!'

'Really?' asked Mickey.

'Affirmative,' said Hildegarde. 'Oh, wait, I just need to get the turning here.' She made Ms Mildred brake suddenly, stopping just before the main roundabout and instead taking a dirt track that most people would have missed if they hadn't been looking.

'Thomasina lives down here?' asked Mickey. It didn't look very residential.

'Perfect for an old spy,' said Hildegarde. 'I remember when she found this place, she said it was hidden in plain sight so she could get around easily, but only those who knew would be able to find it. Try that gate over there?'

Astrid leaned out of the car and lifted the catch. The team drove through, only to be confronted by a paddock completely enclosed by a thick hedge.

'Maybe she's moved?' asked Mickey. Hildegarde got out of the car and shook her head.

'Oh, she'll be here, we just need to look harder. Come along!'

She took five large paces down the eastern side of the paddock, then reached her hand through the hedgerow and seemed to be searching for something.

'I'm sure it's right about here,' said Hildegarde. 'Oh bother, I hope I've got the right tree.'

'What are we looking for?' asked Mickey as she and Astrid both joined in, feeling around inside the hedge. Mickey could feel the wet leaves and spiky ends of branches grazing her wrists.

'It's like a doorknob,' said Hildegarde. 'It might feel like a stubborn old piece of tree.'

Mickey swept her arms around as much as she could, then yelped in surprise as her left hand collided with an old bit of tree, shaped a bit like a handle.

'If I had found it what would do I do next?' she asked cautiously.

'Two turns to the left then one to the right,' said Hildegarde.

Mickey made the movement then they
heard a grinding noise. Hildegarde came to
stand behind her and tapped the hedge with
her umbrella. This time it swung forwards
like a gate to reveal a large sweeping drive
leading to a long thin bungalow that was
made of dark brown wood and covered in
tangles of ivy. It looked more like a bird
hide than a home but Hildegarde smiled and
rubbed her hands together.

'Astrid, please close the gate behind us,

we wouldn't want to let any trespassers in.
Mickey, let's go, and remember to keep your
wits about you; we don't know what exactly
we're walking into. Harry could be close.'

Hildegarde walked up to the door and
knocked gently. The door opened a crack and
a long thin face peered out at them.

'Tommi! It's me,' said Hildegarde. 'Are you
quite alright?'

'I'm so sorry,' said the person behind the
door. 'I've got no idea who you are.'

Chapter
16

'Maybe this is a test?' said Mickey. 'Is there something you can tell her that only you and she know?'

Thomasina had shut the door in their faces and Hildegarde was looking at it thoughtfully. 'I suppose . . .' she said, squaring up to ring the doorbell again. 'Tommi, come back, I have more news for you!'

The letter box opened a crack and the voice came through, 'Look, I don't know what you're doing here, please go away. This is private property. If you don't leave I will have no option but to release the hounds.'

Mickey saw Astrid look around nervously.

'Fishsticks,' said Hildegarde clearly.

'I beg your pardon?' said the voice.

'Fishsticks,' repeated Hildegarde.

'And red hippos in a tree.'

'Hildegarde?' said the voice. The door swung open and there was Thomasina in a long housecoat and tartan slippers.

'It *is* you! I hope you understand that I had to check. You can never be too careful—disguises can be so convincing these days.' She smiled. 'Do come in.'

'Are there really red hippos?' whispered Astrid in Mickey's ear. Mickey was wondering the same thing and threw a quizzical look at Hildegarde.

'Our emergency code words,' said Hildegarde smoothly. 'Haven't needed to use them in years. Tommi, may I introduce you to my friend Mickey.' Hildegarde pushed Mickey forward to shake the hand Thomasina had extended to her. 'I know, I know, she's young but so were we once! I give you my word that she can be trusted. She's one of the most gifted spies I've ever worked with.'

Tommi smiled and greeted Mickey, who could feel herself glowing with pride. They followed Thomasina through to her sitting room.

'I'll cut to the chase since time is of the essence,' Hildegarde began. 'Do you remember Harry Raynott?'

Thomasina frowned but shook her head. 'The name rings a bell but I can't picture him. Perhaps I've seen it on a file?'

'Well,' said Hildegarde, 'he applied for a job with **The Espionage Agency** and we turned him down. It now seems that, unfortunately, he has tracked down the last remaining hard copy with the identities of the five founding members and is seemingly out for revenge. Marjorie and Samira are missing, and we believe he broke into my house though I managed to give him the slip. Have you seen anyone suspicious near your house lately?'

Thomasina rested her chin in her hands

and thought. 'Well, there was someone going round in circles in the paddock earlier in the week, but I'm afraid I assumed it was a delivery driver following one of those GPS trackers.'

'Yes, yes, people end up in ditches and all sorts,' said Hildegarde. 'However, it may have been Harry, and he may be back, so until this situation is under control, I advise moving out to a safe house so he won't know where to find you.'

'What does he want with us though?' asked Thomasina.

'Leverage, I suspect,' said Hildegarde. 'He may be holding the other spies to ransom to try and extract secrets about their work and **The Espionage Agency** and sell it to the highest bidder.'

'This sounds like a matter of national security,' said Thomasina. 'Have you spoken to **The Espionage Agency** yet?'

'Not yet,' said Hildegarde. 'We wanted to check on you first, and another team is looking for Patrick as we speak.'

'Who are you working with, if not **The Espionage Agency**?' asked Thomasina curiously.

'Now Tommi, you know better than to ask something like that,' said Hildegarde. 'Loose lips sink ships and all that.'

Mickey felt a warm glow. Hildegarde was keeping the **COBRA** secret!

'Anyway,' Hildegarde continued, 'time is rather of the essence.'

'Yes,' said Thomasina, 'well, I am still in contact with some people at the Agency. I can head there now and get them up to speed. Will you check on Patrick?'

'We have a team on it, but we'll go to them now and meet you at the Agency later on. Best of luck, my old friend,' said Hildegarde.

'And to you,' said Thomasina. 'Just like old times.'

'Old times indeed!' said Hildegarde. 'Come on Mickey, let's go!'

Chapter

17

'Hildegarde, watch the speed limit!' cried
Mickey as they zipped along the road.

'We have no time to lose! The others may
need our help. I know these roads like the
back of my han—*whoaaa! Hold on!*' Hildegarde
cried, as they swerved around a tight bend.
Astrid looked pointedly at Hildegarde's
driving gloves and went to sit under Mickey's
seat where it felt safer.

Hildegarde didn't use a Sat Nav but she
seemed to be referring to an imaginary one
in her head. Mickey could hear her muttering
instructions to herself: left, second right, then
a bridge. When they approached a restaurant
in the middle of the countryside called *The
Walk Inn,* Hildegarde cried 'ah-hah!', spun Ms
Mildred around an ornamental duck pond,
and came to a stop outside a sweet-looking
thatched cottage.

There was a long path
up to the cottage,
neatly lined
with wild
tangles of
holly bushes.
'Keep your
wits about
you,' said Hildegarde. 'Patrick's
speciality was inventions, so his
house may have all sorts of unusual security
features. We will need to muster all our
cunning to get through them.'

'Or maybe not,' said Astrid from her spot
on Mickey's back. 'Look, the door's open.'

'That doesn't seem good!' cried
Mickey, sprinting towards the
front door. Coby and Rupert had
taken on the task of tracking
down Patrick, but there
was no sign of them
here either.

'Eugh, what's that?'

cried Astrid, as a foul stench suddenly hit their nostrils. They all stopped dead in their tracks.

'Something bad,' said Hildegarde. 'Quickly, cover your noses.' She pulled her own blouse up over her nose and mouth, Mickey did the same and Astrid covered her nose with her tail.

Mickey gingerly pushed the door open and the smell grew even stronger. Hildegarde began bustling around, opening windows and calling for Patrick. 'Coby? Rupert?' Mickey added, looking desperately around for them.

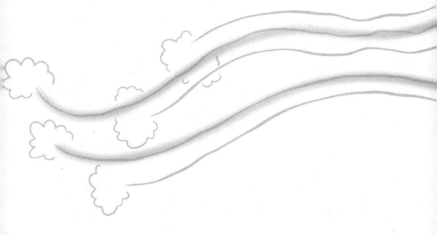

Then, suddenly Mickey saw the unmistakable shape of the end of Coby's tail behind a sofa. 'Coby?' she cried, diving towards the sofa. 'Hildegarde, Astrid, come and help!'

The snake was lying seemingly unconscious on the ground, with Rupert beside her, also out cold.

Hildegarde came charging towards them fanning a newspaper frantically. 'I think the smell is some kind of gas that's been released here. We should all get outside immediately!'

Mickey scooped up Coby, Astrid lifted Rupert, and they all raced out to the garden at the back of the cottage. They carefully laid them down in the garden, hoping the fresh air would help. Hildegarde came running out with two dishes of water and knelt down to drip some of the cool liquid over Coby's mouth. Mickey did the same to Rupert and felt a huge rush of relief as they started to stir.

'Everything's going to be alright,' said Astrid soothingly. 'Try to drink something.'

'Ouch, my head!' said Rupert slowly. 'What happened?'

'Some sort of gas attack,' said Hildegarde, seriously. 'Did you see Patrick?'

'I . . . think so . . .' said Rupert. 'It's all a bit of a blur. We got here and could hear a commotion, so we climbed in through a window to observe but saw an unconscious human being dragged away by a shadowy figure. I'm certain it was Harry. We were about to sound the alarm when I remember feeling very sleepy.'

'It sounds as though Harry used a sleeping gas to knock Patrick off guard, then the effects also got to Coby and Rupert!' said Mickey.

'Let's take them back to HQ,' said Astrid. 'We've now got three missing spies and Harry is still on the loose. Who knows what could happen next if he isn't stopped?'

Chapter

18

Once Coby had recovered her faculties, she was absolutely furious at being temporarily incapacitated. She'd urgently called a meeting back at HQ, permitting Hildegarde to attend as well.

'High Committee,' she hissed. 'Firstly my thanks to Hildegarde, Mickey, and Astrid, whose quick thinking quite possibly saved my life, and Rupert's.' The snake paused to nod at them. Mickey noticed that after the events at Patrick's house, Coby seemed to have softened to Hildegarde's presence. 'However,' Coby continued, 'Harry has taken this too far. This time, I fear it will take more than our combined resources to stop him, so we are left with little option but to head deep into human territory. This could be dangerous, so Mickey, I trust that you have a plan?'

'Yes,' said Mickey. 'We need to head to the headquarters of **The Espionage Agency**. When Astrid, Hildegarde, and I found Thomasina, she said she'd go to see them and brief them about Harry. She asked us to join her once we'd checked on Patrick. If we can find a way to use their resources without letting them know about **COBRA**, that will give us the best chance of finding Harry.'

'And that's where I come in,' said Hildegarde. 'Mickey has done a fine job of protecting your identities, and I will help her to make sure your best interests are protected.'

'So we must head into the city,' said Coby, 'to stop Harry once and for all. Astrid, Clarke, Rupert, you'll be coming with us. Tilda, I need you to stay here in case something happens to the rest of us, and to run any operation as needed from our HQ.'

Tilda nodded.

Bertie's head came into the room. 'A mission into the city? Can I come?'

'I don't think so Bertie, you are too big and will draw attention,' said Coby. Mickey watched the giraffe's face fall and had an idea.

'The thing about the city,' she said, 'is that people tend to be very busy and don't look that closely—so as long as Bertie wears a coat, hat, and a *very* long scarf he should be okay. Especially if he sticks to the shadows.'

Coby sighed. 'I suppose Bertie could come if he does as you suggest, Mickey.'

'I won't let you down!' said Bertie solemnly, and he dashed off to get ready.

Mickey and Astrid helped Bertie to wind a scarf around his neck and Mickey carefully

secured it with
a pin.

'You're going
to do brilliantly,
Bertie,' she said.

'I'm so pleased
I'm coming,' he said
excitedly.

'Of course, we don't
leave any being—including
giraffes—behind,' said
Mickey.

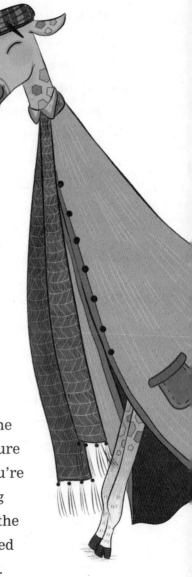

She turned and saw Coby
watching her from further
down the corridor.

'I was just thinking how
far you've come since you
first showed up here,' said the
snake. 'At first we weren't sure
about you at all, but now you're
running missions, mentoring
Bertie, and drawing us into the
human world.' Coby appraised
Mickey with an intense look.

Mickey wasn't quite sure if Coby thought that was a good thing or not, but she didn't have time to ask a follow-up question as Coby moved into marshalling mode.

'Ready, everyone?' she hissed.

'Ready!' they chorused.

'Excellent,' said Coby. 'Now remember team, in the human world we need to be extremely careful. Rupert and Clarke, you shouldn't attract too much suspicion, but remember, strangely, there are places where cats and rats are not welcome. Keep your wits about you. Astrid, you will be in disguise on Hildegarde's back as a novelty backpack, and I shall travel on Mickey's back inside her actual backpack.'

Mickey held out her bag as Coby slithered in, then hoisted it onto her shoulders. She felt Coby's head slide out and position itself just under the hood of her coat so she could hiss quietly to her if a situation arose.

'Tilda and Maura, you will stay at HQ in case anything needs to be coordinated from base, and also to sound the alarm if we are not back by the appointed hour,' Coby commanded from inside the bag. 'Let's go!'

'Good luck, Hildegarde,' said Mickey, as they prepared to set off.

'Luck has nothing to do with it, my dear,' said Hildegarde. 'It's talent, hard work and good brains we need, and luckily you have those in spades.'

Mickey hugged the compliments to her, and they were even enough to distract her from Hildegarde's driving as the two humans and their undercover animal spies set off on their way into the city. Rupert and Clarke were in the front passenger seat talking to Hildegarde, while Mickey sat next to Coby, Astrid, and Bertie in the back seat with a blanket on her lap which she was ready to throw over them, should any humans stop to peer into their car.

'Ah here we are!' cried Hildegarde eventually, as Ms Mildred screeched to a halt. 'Everyone, stick with me. If anyone notices anything untoward, rest assured I shall throw them off the scent and protect you, and I'm sure Mickey will too.'

Mickey nodded fiercely.

Hildegarde led the way to a grand office building that looked like it was made entirely out of glass, on the edge of a smart square. There was a uniformed doorman outside and Mickey could see security checkpoints in the building's reception too.

'I'll wait outside and run surveillance on the street,' whispered Bertie, heading to a patch of trees where he could disguise his height among their low-hanging branches.

'Good idea,' approved Coby.

'Oh my, isn't it grand!' whispered Astrid. 'Far fancier than our shed!'

But Hildegarde didn't take them into the gleaming foyer. Instead, she swerved and marched into a minicab office next door.

'The main entrance is just for show,' Hildegarde whispered to Mickey. 'This is the secret way in—follow my lead.' Mickey nodded and looked around to check all the animals were still with them and bent down to scoop Rupert up and put him in her pocket.

'Hello George, good to see you!' Hildegarde

called cheerily to the man operating the phones. 'Just popping in to use the facilities.' She took Mickey's arm and led her towards the staff toilets at the back of the room, waited for Clarke to follow, and closed the door behind them. She then walked to the third stall, ignored the large

'OUT OF ORDER'

sign that was pasted on the door and instead reached in and pulled the old-fashioned flush. Mickey gasped as the toilet vanished and a corridor appeared in its place.

'Oh, this *is* like our shed!' said Astrid. 'Only without the goldfish!'

Hildegarde grinned. 'It is astonishing, the similarities, when both organizations have evolved completely independently of each other. Ah, now we're nearly inside **The Espionage Agency's** headquarters, we just need to go through security.'

Mickey looked around and saw that they were now in the security checkpoints she'd seen in the grand building. 'Anyone who comes to the regular entrance gets turned away,' Hildegarde whispered. 'Now, if you've got the rat I'll carry the dear cat.'

'Actually, I'll take Clarke,' said Mickey quickly, wanting Clarke where she could keep a firm eye on him. Hildegarde nodded and then, together with her Astrid backpack, headed towards security.

Mickey held out her arms and Clarke allowed himself to be scooped up. Mickey and the animal spies followed Hildegarde, who was now chatting to the security staff.

'And this is Mickey, and her pet cat.'

'Oh, I do love cats,' said the guard, 'and this one is a beauty.'

'We don't usually let pets in, as you well know Ms McTavish,' said the tallest guard, 'but we'll make an honourable exception seeing as it's you!'

They were escorted into a plush lift and

shown into the fanciest meeting room Mickey had ever seen. Everything gleamed and the walls were covered with expensive-looking paintings. The security guard left, promising that someone would be with them shortly, and Rupert climbed out of Mickey's pocket and scurried over to get a closer look at the art.

Suddenly there was a commotion in the corridor outside and Mickey saw agents racing past their room on the way down the corridor. It looked like something big had happened, but no one stopped at their door to tell them what.

'Come on,' motioned Hildegarde, gesturing to the doorway. Together they slipped down the corridor and peered through a wall of potted plants to see if they could see what was going on.

'How lovely, a
Monstera deliciosa,'
said Hildegarde
stroking one of the
leaves.

'A delicious

monster?' asked Mickey.

'No, a Swiss cheese plant,' said Hildegarde, 'so-named because of the holes in its leaves—see?'

Mickey did, and joined Hildegarde to peer through the leaves, trying desperately to see what was going on.

'Someone's coming, quickly, back in the room!' said Hildegarde suddenly.

The pair sprinted back into their meeting room just in time as a young agent in a smart dark suit with a curly wired earpiece appeared in the doorway.

'Hildegarde McTavish? What a pleasure to meet you,' he said, coming into the room. 'Thomasina told us we might be seeing you, with a special guest today.' The guard looked over at Mickey. 'And so this must be Mickey?'

'That's right,' Hildegarde said, prodding her forward.

'Pleased to meet you,' said Mickey politely, shaking the extended hand of the mysterious agent.

'Please, follow me,' he said, leading the way

down the corridor to a door marked 'Broom Cupboard'.

BROOM CUPBOARD

But, when the door opened it wasn't a storeroom at all. Instead, it was the highest spec meeting room Mickey had ever seen. The wall was tiled with computer screens of different sizes. Some showed graphs and charts, some showed CCTV from the street outside, and some showed serious-looking adults calling in their briefings from elsewhere in the world. In the middle of the room was a gleaming silver table, and sitting in the seats placed around it were a dozen unsmiling agents, with Thomasina sitting at the end of the table next to a smartly dressed woman wearing dark sunglasses.

'Welcome to the most secure meeting room in the world,' whispered Hildegarde.

'This is the secret headquarters of **The Espionage Agency**.'

Everyone nodded at Hildegarde as she stood before them, and Mickey desperately tried to look as though she also belonged even though she suddenly felt very out of her depth indeed.

'Mickey, Hildegarde,' said Thomasina, rising to her feet, 'please allow me to introduce the current High Committee of **The Human Espionage Agency** led by the brilliant Ms Mira DuPont.' She indicated the woman next to her who also rose and reached out to shake Hildegarde's hand and then Mickey's.

'Pleased to meet you,' she said politely. 'Ms McTavish, it is an honour.'

Hildegarde nodded then cut straight to the chase. 'Have you been briefed on Harry Raynott?' she asked.

'We've just received a tape,' said Mira gravely. 'We think it's the missing agents. Harry has them.'

Chapter
19

'Roll the tape,' said Hildegarde.

The agent seated at the console pressed play and Mickey jumped as Harry's snarling face filled the screen.

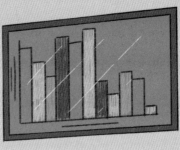

'So, you think you're *so* clever do you?'
he said. 'Well, not only did I find the folder
revealing the identities of the original
Espionage Agency, but I've kidnapped three of
your original spies. And if you don't believe
me, here they are . . .' The camera suddenly
swung around and showed Marjorie, Samira,
and Patrick lined up against a wall. Their
mouths and hands were bound and they were
all blinking furiously.

'My friends!' gasped Hildegarde.

'So now you have to choose,' said Harry. 'I want $5 million in cryptocurrency sent to my account—I'll send you the details. If you don't do it, not only will I leave these three tied up where you can't find them, and trust me, they won't last long here, but I will also make sure the world knows you were very happy to leave your friends to die when you had the chance to save them. You have three hours to arrange the funds. Tick-tock . . .'

The feed changed to a link to purchase the anonymous online currency he was after, and Harry disappeared from view.

'Can we get a read on his location?' asked the agent at the head of the table.

'IT are trying to trace the location, but he's using software to bypass the usual servers,' replied an agent by the screen. 'Right now, it's showing up as an island on the other side of the world, which isn't likely. They can get the right location but it's going to take time.'

'Which we don't have,' said Hildegarde. 'We need to put all our resources into it. This is a category one incident.'

'Can I see the message again?' asked
Mickey, as all the adults turned to look at her.

'Does anyone else want to see it again?'
asked the agent at the console, looking to
Mira for approval.

'Follow Mickey's hunch,' said Mira. 'Play it
again.'

The junior agent shrugged and pressed the
tape again. Mickey looked closely at the three
captives. They were all blinking furiously.
Mickey thought carefully about what she
would do in their position while watching
them closely for patterns. Then she was hit by
a sudden realization.

'Oh!' she exclaimed. 'I think they're
blinking Morse code.'

The agent paused the film and zoomed
in on Samira's eyes then began translating
the blinks into long and short Morse code
symbols on an interactive white board.

• — • / • • / • • • — / • / • — •

Short–Long–Short, Short–Short,
Short–Short–Short–Long, Short,
Short–Long–Short

Then Marjorie:

— • • • / • — • / • • / — • • / — — • / •

Long–Short–Short–Short, Short–
Long–Short, Short–Short, Long–
Short–Short, Long–Long–Short,
Short

And finally Patrick:

— — • / • — • / • — / • • — • /

• • — • / • • / — / • •

Long–Long–Short, Short–Long–
Short, Short–Long, Short–Short–
Long–Short, Short–Short–
Long–Short, Short–Short, Long,
Short–Short

Morse code

A	•—	M	——	Y	—•——
B	—•••	N	—•	Z	——••
C	—•—•	O	———	0	—————
D	—••	P	•——•	1	•————
E	•	Q	——•—	2	••———
F	••—•	R	•—•	3	•••——
G	——•	S	•••	4	••••—
H	••••	T	—	5	•••••
I	••	U	••—	6	—••••
J	•———	V	•••—	7	——•••
K	—•—	W	•——	8	———••
L	•—••	X	—••—	9	————•

'Oh, well-spotted Mickey!' said Hildegarde, who was fluent in Morse. 'Do you want to tell them what it says?'

'River, Bridge, Graffiti,' said Mickey.

'Get the team on it and start searching the area!' said Hildegarde. 'Excellent job, Mickey!'

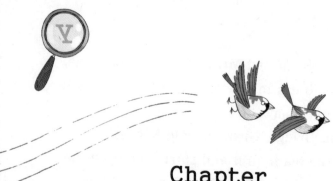

Chapter

20

'What will they do now?' Mickey asked
Hildegarde, as the other agents raced out of
the room, and Mickey and Hildegarde headed
back to their original room where Clarke,
Astrid, Coby, and Rupert were waiting.

'They'll start sweeping the area, looking
for a river with a bridge covered in graffiti.
They'll triangulate the signals from Harry's
video with the area around the river—the
Morse code hints really help to narrow
down the possible options. Though I suppose
there are a lot of bridges over rivers . . .'
Hildegarde trailed off.

'But are they moving quickly enough?'

Mickey asked. 'Harry gave them three hours and by my watch we've lost 20 minutes already. Time isn't on our side so we need to find them quickly. If only . . . oh, I have an idea!' Mickey

ran out onto the balcony and whistled, watching in delight as a robin, two sparrows, and a blackbird came soaring in to land. This hadn't been authorized by Coby, but there wasn't any time to waste.

'We're looking for a location that includes a bridge, a river, and graffiti. Look for any buildings where someone could be hiding out nearby. Please ask as many birds to help as you can and report back—it's extremely important and

it's a matter of life and death!'

The birds nodded, spread their wings, and shot off into the sky.

Mickey paced the balcony, anxiously scanning the skies and watching cars full of human agents leaving from the building's underground car park. She knew that Thomasina and Mira—the head of the human spy network—were working on tracking Harry's call, and the other agents were out on the road searching for the missing spies. She looked back into the room where Hildegarde and Coby were speaking in hushed tones, and then Mickey's attention was drawn to a soaring robin heading directly towards her.

'There's an old dilapidated boathouse down by the river a couple of miles west from here,' it cried, not even waiting until it had landed. 'I think that's the place you need! It's next to a footbridge, and some of the birds nearby heard sounds of human shouts earlier, and there are signs of a scuffle in the mud! The next building along is called something like an "ice arena"?'

'Excellent job,' said Mickey running in to tell the others. 'I think they're being held in the boathouse by the ice arena. Let's tell the Agency!'

But Hildegarde grimaced. 'Time is running out. I can think of no better team than **COBRA** to go to the scene. The tip-off came from one of your own, after all. I'll stay here and try to persuade Mira to focus her agents' efforts on this area of the river and hopefully see you there.'

'We won't let you down!' said Mickey quickly, then she turned to the assembled animal spies. 'Rupert, come into my pocket,' she said, lifting the rat into the hiding place. 'Astrid, on my back please. Coby you can travel inside my bag, and Clarke . . .' The cat looked up at her. 'I'll hold you, but you'll have to be tucked inside my jacket, is that okay?'

'Since you asked nicely, I'll allow it,' said Clarke.

'Good luck!' called Hildegarde as they headed down the corridor, Mickey retracing her steps until they were back outside in the fresh air.

'There's the robin!' said Mickey, pointing to where it was waiting, ready to show them the way to the boathouse.

'And Bertie!' whispered Astrid, pointing with her paw.

Mickey could see Bertie was still standing patiently where they had left him when they'd first arrived, still on duty in case he was needed. He was still wrapped up in his commuter disguise and had positioned himself next to a pair of tall trees, his long neck camouflaged by their branches. When he saw Mickey he nodded smartly then began following her, keeping to the shadowy side of the street.

Together, Mickey and the animal spies followed the robin along the city's winding streets as they drew closer to the ice arena.

'I used to come here with my parents,' said Mickey, 'but it shut down years ago.' When

they had reached the abandoned ice rink
they followed the river until Mickey cried,

'There!
    Look!'
       and pointed.

'Is that the boathouse?' Bertie asked.
'I think so,' she whispered back. She could

see the shadowy outline of the old boathouse,
nestled next to the river and sitting alongside
a footbridge that was covered in graffiti.
Could this be the place?

'What do we do
now?' asked Bertie.
'I don't know yet,' Mickey
said, her brain racing, 'but if
the missing spies are in there we
need to find a safe way to get them
out, and quickly!'

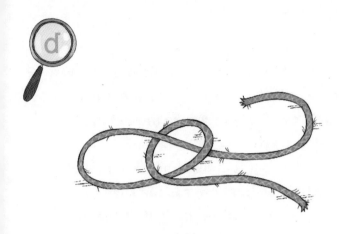

Chapter

21

'I have an idea,' whispered Bertie as they snuck around the outside of the building. 'There's a skylight on the roof which is slightly open—so while to a human it looks like a secured building, to a giraffe . . . well, I see a potential way in. I could help one of you up so you can see what's going on inside the building.'

'That's a great idea, Bertie!' Mickey whispered. 'Let's try it!' She spotted a coil of rope lying near the wall, picked it up, and gave it a shake. 'I have an idea too. I can use this rope to lower myself down, and then perhaps I can find out where in the building the hostages are.'

'I'll find a spot to hide in and keep watch,' said Bertie, nodding towards the shadows.

'No,' said Coby, slithering out of the tote bag and onto Mickey's shoulder. 'We need you with us. Your height and strength might come in handy if we need to confront Harry. I'll go with Mickey to help her look. The rest of you can wait for my signal together, and I'm sure it goes without saying, but stay on full alert for any signs of danger.'

The giraffe beamed with pride at being included in their plan, and turned to Mickey. 'Come on then you two, climb aboard!'

Coby wound herself loosely around Mickey's neck while she wrapped the rope around her waist. Then she climbed onto Bertie's back and up his neck, holding on tightly as he manoeuvred Mickey and Coby towards the open skylight. Mickey gingerly stepped from Bertie onto the old roof. It gave a creak underneath her weight and made Mickey gasp.

Mickey looked through the skylight but the room beneath seemed to be deserted. Very carefully, she tied one end of the rope around the handle of the skylight and the other end around her waist. Mickey lowered herself and Coby down into the room below, thanking her lucky stars that they'd practised rope climbing in her gymnastics classes. As they inched lower to the ground, Mickey noticed two doors, one at either end of the room. Was Harry behind one of them? And were Samira, Marjorie, and Patrick there too?

Mickey dropped to the floor and untied the rope from around her waist, then watched as the rope slithered upwards, pulled by Astrid to remove the evidence that there was now someone else inside the boathouse. Just in case, she crept to the corner of the room and hid herself behind a dusty canoe while she listened carefully. She could hear the sound of loud footsteps pacing back and forth behind the door to her right. They sounded horribly like the heavy tread she had heard at Hildegarde's house.

This had to be Harry, Mickey thought. It was just possible that the hostages were behind the other door on the left. Mickey made eye contact with Coby and nodded over at the door to their left. Coby slithered down to the ground, and together they crept towards the door. Mickey tried the handle and gave the door a gentle push. Slowly, the door swung open and they entered the room, closing it softly behind them. It was dimly lit and scattered with old boats and outdoor equipment that had seen better days. The main entrance to the boathouse was on the far side of the room, secured tightly shut with a heavy padlock and chain, and in the middle of the room, tied to the wooden posts that were holding up the roof, were the missing spies!

Patrick, Samira, and Marjorie were slumped on the floor, their arms and legs bound together with rope and their mouths

covered so they couldn't shout for help. A
video camera on a tripod was positioned
directly in front of them. Mickey signalled
to Coby who slithered over and turned it off,
staying out of sight of the hostages. Mickey
held both hands up, hoping to signal to the
spies that she meant no harm and then
rushed over to Samira who was the nearest.

'It's okay, I'm with Hildegarde,' she
whispered, as she loosened the ropes and
removed the mouth gag. 'Are you okay?'

'Much better for seeing you,' said Samira,
tilting her head and rubbing her wrists where
the ropes had cut in.

'Can you stand?' Mickey asked anxiously,
as she removed the ropes around Samira's
feet, noticing that she was wincing.

'I'll be okay, we just have to be quick!' she
said. 'He'll be back soon. If you can help me
over to Patrick, I'll sort his ropes while you
get Marjorie's.'

Mickey did as she was told—there was no
time to waste. Just as they were all almost
free, Mickey heard those dreaded footsteps

once more. And it sounded as though they were getting closer.

'No time to run,' whispered Mickey. 'We'll have to pretend you are still tied up. Don't worry—we're expecting backup any moment.' Mickey helped the spies put the covers over their mouths again. They quickly got back into position and placed their hands behind their backs, kicking the ropes out of sight, and hoping that Harry wouldn't notice that their feet were no longer bound in the dim light. Mickey dived behind the wreck of an old boat, and Coby slithered to her side.

'Only 20 minutes left on the clock and nothing in the account yet. Time to make another video, I think,' a voice said, as the door swung open and a man entered the room. Mickey knew that voice and watched, her heart thumping, as Harry strode around the room just metres away from her and Coby. Luckily, he wasn't looking too closely at the spies, and Mickey hoped beyond hope that he wouldn't notice they were no longer tied to the posts as he'd left them.

But then, from nowhere, Mickey felt the unmistakable feeling of a sneeze growing in her nose. It could not have come at a worse time. She tried rubbing her nose and she tried blinking frantically, but nothing could keep the sneeze down and

suddenly

it came rushing out.

ATISSHOOOOo!

Chapter

Mickey tried to scoot under the boat, hoping Harry wouldn't look there, but she wasn't quick enough and suddenly felt the bright light of Harry's torch shining into her face.

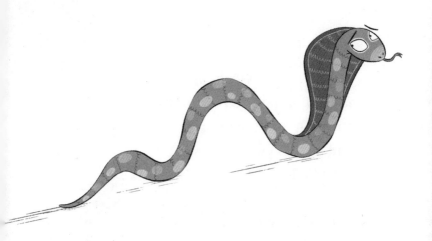

'Hey!' he cried. 'Wait . . . I know you!
You're the kid who hangs around with
COBRA, doing my old job.'

'Hi, Harry,' said Mickey, waving her arms
to distract him to give Coby enough time
to hide herself in the shadows.

'What are you doing here?'
he demanded. 'Come
to join forces
with me?'

'No!'

cried Mickey in horror. 'I'm here to rescue the agents,' she said, trying to sound a lot bolder than she actually felt, 'and to

stop you!'

Harry laughed. 'You've come to stop me? But you're just a kid. And it looks like you came alone. Big mistake.'

Just then, there was an almighty crash and Harry staggered back, throwing his torch beam at the main door.

'Who says she's alone?' Bertie yelled indignantly, as he came charging through the main door, sending the padlock flying and coming to a stop in front of Harry, towering over him

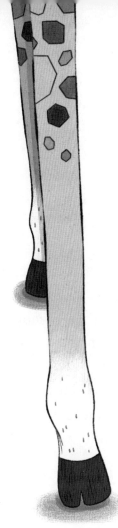

threateningly.

Glad to have the giraffe standing between her and Harry, Mickey rushed over to the captives. They were still pretending to be tied to the wall but now their eyes were as wide as saucers. How would she explain that they had just been saved by a giraffe?

'Hello Bertie,' said Harry smoothly, picking up a rope from the floor and running it through his hands.

'Shouldn't you be behind a desk somewhere?'

Harry advanced on Bertie who turned and began to run in a zigzag motion around the room. 'You'll have to catch me first!' he cried, as Harry chased furiously after him.

Mickey signalled frantically to Patrick,

Marjorie, and Samira to try to sneak out the main door while Harry was distracted by Bertie. The spies nodded and began to slip away, the loosened ties still in their hands. Mickey looked back at Bertie and Harry, and noticed that while Bertie had been giving Harry the run-around, Clarke, Astrid, and Rupert had also crept into the room and were hiding behind an old canoe that was lying on the ground. Mickey could also see the shadow of the end of Coby's tail near the boat so knew the snake was nearby.

'As if you're actually going to stop me,' snarled Harry. He slowed down and tied the rope into a lasso, swinging it round his head. Bertie stopped, looking anxious.

'Human spies, animal spies, you all think you're so clever,' said Harry, eyeing up Bertie with a cruel look on his face. 'You know I tried to use my skills to help you, but **The Espionage Agency** wouldn't have me and **COBRA** never truly appreciated my genius and then replaced me with a mere child! I knew I was far cleverer than the lot of you put together, and when I unmask the original agents and the existence of **COBRA**, finally, the whole world will know how brilliant I am!

'I've outsmarted **COBRA** before and now I'll do it again. I see now that **The Espionage Agency** was never going to pay me the ransom, but it's been fun throwing the whole agency into turmoil, so I think I'll leave these three here so they'll know they could have been saved if only their current agents were just a little bit smarter. I don't suppose anyone will even notice there's a child and a giraffe in here as well until I'm safely out of the country.

'And want to know the best part? There's nothing any of you can do about it!' he cackled, swinging his rope towards Bertie who ducked it expertly so Harry missed.

Mickey didn't agree there was nothing they could do to stop him—once again, Harry had vastly underestimated the collective power of Mickey and the animal spies.

Mickey watched as Astrid made a leap for the light switch, plunging the room into complete

darkness.

The only light
now was from
Harry's torch
lying on the
floor.

Mickey dashed over to help. Coby slithered over with Astrid and Clarke to help pin Harry to the ground.

Patrick, Samira, and Marjorie took advantage of the darkness, doubled back into the room and ran back towards Harry, swiftly tying the ropes that had held them captive around their captor.

'Noooo, let me go you *brutes*,' groaned Harry, as he struggled and tried to break free.

'We did it!' cried Mickey. 'This means . . .' but she was interrupted by the sound of more people arriving. 'Hide!' whispered Mickey as she, Coby, Clarke, Astrid, Rupert, and Bertie darted behind the old boats. Patrick, Samira, and Marjorie stayed where they were, keeping a firm hold of Harry.

'It's me,' came
Hildegarde's voice, as
she ran up and flicked
the lights on. She was
accompanied by a squad
of human agents led by
Mira, the Head of **The
Espionage Agency**.

Harry groaned from where he was lying bound on the floor. 'Mira!' he shouted. 'This is a terrible mistake. The place is surrounded by animal spies, they're highly dangerous and *they* were the ones who kidnapped the agents and forced me to make that video with their ransom demands—they were framing me to take the fall. Arrest them all, I'm on your side, the side of **The Espionage Agency**, and we are in

terrible danger

from these beasts!'

'Oh, I don't think so, Harry Raynott,' said Mira. 'You've caused quite enough mayhem and will be going away for quite some time now.'

Hildegarde darted over to Samira, Marjorie, and Patrick. Mickey had been worried they might be shaken by their time in the boathouse, but their eyes were shining and Mickey could hear Patrick saying the rescue had made him feel twenty years younger as they were led outside to safety by a team of human agents.

Harry, on the other hand, refused to go quietly. It took seven agents to wrestle him out of the boathouse and into the waiting car outside.

'The thing is,' said Hildegarde to Mira as they watched the agents leave, 'what Harry said was half-true. He wasn't in terrible danger but—' Mickey stared at Hildegarde in horror as she added, 'but the place *is* surrounded by animal spies.'

'No!' cried Mickey, running out from behind the boat to face Hildegarde.

'I trusted you!'

Mickey's heart sank as she knew Hildegarde's betrayal meant the end of her time with **COBRA**. Coby and the others would never forgive her. And after Hildegarde had betrayed her trust, she would never forgive *her* either. Mickey could feel tears welling up in her eyes and blinked furiously to hold them back.

Coby wriggled forwards towards Hildegarde and Mira, and hissed loudly. Mira jumped straight into the air in fright.

'You need to get out of here!' Mickey cried. 'Hildegarde has blown your cover!'

'It's okay, Mickey,' said Hildegarde in her cool, calm voice. 'This is Coby, the Head of **COBRA**. Coby, this is Mira, the Head of **The Espionage Agency**.'

Hildegarde turned to Mickey. 'Coby and I made a plan while you were coordinating the bird searches and decided that while we certainly couldn't tell the whole agency about **COBRA**, we could make an exception for Mira.'

'So it is really true? This is really

173

happening?' said Mira looking at Coby curiously.

'It is,' said Coby, and Mira sank to the floor, in a deep faint.

'She'll probably be okay when she wakes up; that happened to me the first time too,' Mickey remembered. 'You're really okay with humans knowing about **COBRA**?' she asked Coby.

'Only a very select group,' said Coby. 'This business with Harry has shown me that there will be some cases where our combined expertise can be more powerful than the sum of its parts. It seems like it is time to take **COBRA** to the next level.'

'Absolutely agreed,' said Hildegarde. 'When Mira wakes up and has come to terms with it, I'm sure she will be happy to make arrangements. And that's the thing about **The Espionage Agency** spies—we're the best at keeping secrets, so your secrets will be safe with us.'

'And that's why Harry could never have joined your ranks,' said Coby.

'Exactly,' said Hildegarde.

'So I'm still part of **COBRA**?' Mickey asked, hardly believing her luck.

'We couldn't do it without you,' said Astrid, coming forward to hold her hand.

'I suppose you do rather liven things up,' came Clarke's voice as he stepped out of his hiding place.

'You're my favourite **COBRA** member! Ah, sorry, Coby,' said Bertie, still desperate to stay on the snake's good side, as he popped his long neck up from behind a sail boat.

'You've done something really quite remarkable,' said Hildegarde. 'I'm sure when Mira wakes up she will also be keen to express her gratitude at the way you've brought together both the animal spy world and the human spy world.'

Mickey couldn't believe what was happening. Finally, she felt seen and understood by both animal spies AND human spies, and it was the best feeling she could have imagined.

Chapter

23

When Mira woke up, the plan worked exactly as Hildegarde had predicted. Mira was astonished by the existence of a network of animal spies, and that animals could talk to humans if they wished, and she was now full of ideas about ways to enhance their undercover operations, together.

COBRA was made into an official government organization and given a whole floor of **The Espionage Agency**'s building for their headquarters. It came complete with high-tech equipment, an individually designed ergonomic chair for each member, a red telephone leading directly to Mira's mobile phone should they need her, and a secret entrance with a private elevator so the team could remain incognito while coming and going.

'I don't think we need to tell the rest of the Agency about **COBRA**, but should you need us we'll be there to help,' she assured Coby.

'But what will everyone think is happening on this floor?' asked Mickey.

'They'll understand it's Top Secret and they can't all know all our secrets,' said Mira. 'And if anyone asks I'll tell them **COBRA** is an acronym. Nobody would ever dream it was actually a group led by a real cobra.'

Coby hissed and nodded her approval. Mickey thought she suited these new surroundings, and knew that the snake and her High Committee were excited about the potential of taking on more cases with the hope of helping more animals *and* humans in the future.

As for Mickey, she liked visiting **COBRA**'s glittering new headquarters, but what she liked best of all was on weekends when she and the rest of the High Committee (including Bertie who had recently been promoted), along with the founding members of **The Espionage Agency**, all gathered at Hildegarde's house for games.

The next Saturday, Mickey watched as Marjorie showed Tilda how to knit, Patrick, Bertie and Rupert were having a long discussion about portraiture and hiding messages in paintings, Samira was chatting to Astrid and Maura in the garden, Clarke had buried himself underneath the sofa to dream of tuna, and Hildegarde and Thomasina were digging out more puzzle books from the old

oak chest where they were stored.

The two worlds were united and Mickey felt at home. She stepped back to take in the scene properly, and her foot nudged against a jigsaw piece that was lying on the rug. As she bent down, she saw it had been neatly camouflaged as the piece was exactly the same shade as the wool. As she turned it over in her hand, she realized she knew exactly where it belonged—it was the last piece of Hildegarde's jigsaw puzzle of Venice. She walked through the house, weaving her way around the collected group of animal spies and human spies and approached the jigsaw. She clicked the missing puzzle piece into place and it fitted perfectly. Looking around at the combination of human spies and animal spies, Mickey beamed. She knew that even when she was as grown-up as Hildegarde, she would remember this feeling because right at that moment,

everything felt perfect.

About the author

Anne Miller grew up in Scotland and now lives in London where she makes TV and radio programmes including BBC Two's *QI* and Radio Four's *The Museum of Curiosity*. She reached the semi-finals of the fiendishly difficult quiz show *Only Connect* and has two *Blue Peter* badges. Her current favourite animal is a puffin.

ANNE MILLER

About the illustrator

BECKA MOOR

Becka Moor is a children's book illustrator living in Manchester. She studied illustration for children's publishing at Glyndwr University, graduating in 2012. Since then, she has worked on a variety of young fiction, non-fiction, and picture books. She has a slight obsession with cats and likes anything a bit on the quirky side.

PUZZLES!

Pigpen Code

Can you decipher these words?

THE KEY ON THE NEXT PAGE WILL HELP!

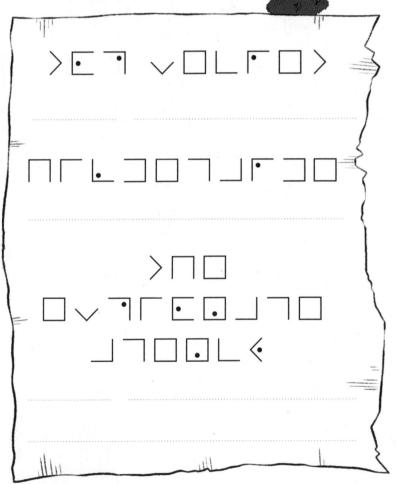

Pigpen Key

Morse Code

Can you read these notes?

_ . _ . / _ _ _ / _ . . . / . _ . / . _

_ . _ . / _ _ _ / _ . / . . _ . / . . / _ . . / . / _ . / _ / . . / . _ _ . / . _ . .

Hidden Code

Did you spot the hidden code within the
magnifying glasses in this book?

Hint: You might want to use a mirror.

Spiral Codes

To read a spiral puzzle, start in the top left hand corner, then read the letter around in a spiral, e.g.

```
C   R   O
L   E   C
I   D   O
```

Can you decipher these codes?

```
B   E              G   O
R   A              T   A
```

```
M   O              J   E   L
L   E              S   H   L
                   I   F   Y
```

```
C  H  A            G  A  L  A
O  N  M            N  G  U  P
E  L  E            E  N  I  A
                   P  S  O  G
```

```
G  R  E  A            D  E
H  A  R  T            R  E
S  S  K  W
E  T  I  H
```

```
                   G  O  L  D
B  U  T            E  V  E  E
L  Y  T            I  S  R  N
F  R  E            R  T  E  R
```

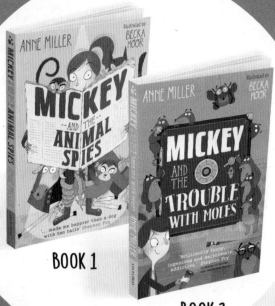

CATCH UP ON PAST ADVENTURES . . .

BOOK 1

BOOK 2

SPECIAL AGENT

COBRA

CONFIDENTIAL

AGENT ID: 139311525

Thank you to Louise Lamont—agent extraordinaire, snack connoisseur and kindred spirit.

To Mickey's brilliant editor Clare Whitston and to Gillian Sore, Kate Penrose, Hannah Penny, Emma Froud, Liz Scott, Eirian Griffiths and everyone at OUP for believing in Mickey.

To Becka Moor—working with you is an absolute dream.

Thank you to Sarah Lloyd, John Lloyd and all of Team QI for making life Quite Interesting.

To Robin Stevens for endless wisdom, James Harkin for fictional financial tips, Emily Jupitus for video wizardry, Ben Moore for code inspiration and to Sara, Mira, Adam, Cynthia and the Puzzled Pinters quiz team.

A huge thank you to my parents and my brother Alasdair for always supporting and encouraging my stories.

To my husband Sam for reading numerous drafts and always believing in my writing.

Special thanks and COBRA salutes to the readers and booksellers who have embraced the world of animal spies.

!KROW TNELLECXE—YEKCIM HTIW GNOLA SELZZUP EHT DEVLOS OHW SREDAER EHT OT UOY KNAHT LAICEPS A DNA

ANNE MILLER